Nine Doors
Foster

There are few heartbreaks as profound as the loss of a friend - a proper friend - who you grew up with and would have done anything for. The reason for this is that they are intrinsically linked, like the music and the fashion of the time, to the period in our lives when we were becoming the people we are. Without them, we would not be exactly who we became. Without them, it's as though a part of us is gone as well.

This book is meant to be daft. Being silly *in* awful situations is what gets us through them, and I think being silly here may just be what reminds someone of a better time, of better people and that they are important to so many more people than they probably realise. This is all about the characters' interactions, so don't expect flamboyant descriptions; do expect profanity and idiocy. Being silly may *prevent* awful situations.

The story here is exactly that: a story. However, almost every character is named after somebody real, and modelled loosely on someone who existed - which absolutely does not mean they did the things written here. The setting, too, is based very much on a real place. The reason for these choices is that this is a real 'story', very close to my heart, and very much part of my world.

Friends are for life - not just for childhood; we may sometimes need reminding of that.

In loving, twisted memory of
Jamie Buck **(2018)** & Lee Hoar **(2019)**

And with immense love for
Ruche van der Mescht
(2012)

Thank you to my amazing wife, Cass, for encouraging me, and to the following beautiful people for their support:

Kev Palmer, Ste Mitchell, Darren Hughes, Marc Holehouse, Lauren Cossey, Phil Tate, Phil Lorenson, Chris Stephenson, Paul Stephenson, Craig Carney, Kelly Laycock, Lyndsay Cullen, Helen Richardson, Andrew Wallace, Sonia Henderson, Claire Brown, Cormac Russell, Jade Wardle, Ashish Patel.

To my daughters, swearing *is* funny when you do it right. Read this at 18.

Prologue

Standing in his way were a group of youths, in their teens. In the dark it was hard to tell what they looked like, and they didn't speak. As one advanced, he turned slightly sideways and raised his back heel, ready to fight.

The glint of moonlight on metal changed his mind for him, and instead he tried to step backward but he had his body in the wrong position.

As the blade entered his abdomen, he saw the eyes of his attacker from within the shadows of its hood: young, scared eyes. A voice somewhere said something, and the blade entered again, then again.

Then, he was alone. As quickly as they had appeared, they were gone. He slid down the wall behind him, his legs splaying out in front of him in a v-shape. He could feel the warm terror drenching his torso and upper legs.

His hands tried to stem the flow, but he felt weak.

To each side he looked, but at this hour nobody would be out walking, and no houses faced directly onto the alleyway.

Alone, and fading, he gasped his last words.

'We should have stayed together…'

Chapter 1: Crem

'Not the best of circumstances, but good to see you mate.'

'Same to you, pal. Where's the rest?'

'Cookie text; said he's parking the car. Gaz is inside already and Kev's having a slash.'

'Where?'

'Here.'

'You can't have a piss out here!'

'Why not?'

'Alright, pussies!'

'Cookie, lad. You keeping alright?'

'Not bad. Been better, obviously!'

'Obviously, yeah.'

'How you two doing?'

'There's three of us!'

'That Kev? What's he doing behind there?'

'He's having a slash!'

'Ah, you can't do that, man.'

'Why not?'

'I've already told him that.'

'It's a fucking crematorium - you can't just piss up the back of it. Where's your respect?'

'It would have been down the inside of my suit leg if I hadn't!'

'Just hurry up, you've been ages behind there!'

'Well you know what it's like when it starts off as a number one...'

'Starts off? Don't tell me you've...'

'I'm having a tab.'

'Think it's no smoking here, Mitch.'

'What, are the bodies going to die again?'

'Look at you wankers. Reservoir Sloths! What a clip, the lot of you!'

'Cheers for that insightful critique. Where've you been?'

'Waiting for Gaz to pick me up, but the daft cunt never showed so I've had to get the bus.'

'Gaz is inside already!'

'What? Ignorant! Fucking pleb!'

'He must have just forgotten; it's a stressful time for everyone isn't it!'

'More stressful when you're sitting next to some teenage streak of piss blasting broken computer noises out of its oversized earmuffs!'

'Its?'

'Can't tell nowadays can you!'

'Bit transphobic, Hughesy!'

'Is it fuck. It's creepy-kid-phobic that's all. Weird little cunts, the lot of them.'

'Lads, lads, lads!'

'Bucky, wondered where you'd got to. Didn't know if you'd even seen the Facebook messages.'

'Just busy, wouldn't miss this for the world. Lads back together...'

'This isn't a social gathering, mate, it's death!'

'Yeah, I know, but still...it's a long time since we've been in one place isn't it. Can only be good times after this bit. Rare we can be sociable nowadays, right?'

'I'm going back to work after this 'bit'.'

'Same here.'

'What? What about you, Hughesy? Kev?'

'Picking kids up from school at three, sorry man!'

'I'm coming to the wake...'

'Yes! One of you isn't a letdown!'

'For an hour then I've got to get home to walk the dog.'

'Is it watching the clock like?'

'Might as well have said you're washing your hair!'

'Hello, gentlemen!'

'Knacker - Bucky wants someone to go on the piss with him!'

'I'd love to, yeah...'

'Well, like...I wanted all of us to be together, not just a fucking gay date with the world's only Rik Waller tribute act!'

'Well, nice - I've got to do the school run today though...didn't take long for the old nicknames and insults to reappear, did it?'

'To be honest, Knacker, I don't know your real name.'

'Same here, pal.'

'Same.'

'Is that Kev? Where the hell is he?'

'He went for a piss behind this hedge and it turned into a shit!'

'That must be really fucking sore!'

'They don't mean my piss literally turned into shit, Dave!'

'Hey, Dave. Last one here, I think. You good?'

'Well apart from the death of my friend and the concern I have for Kev's private parts, I'm plodding along. Gaz isn't here yet!'

'He's inside.'

'I'm not!'

'You, you massive septic flange, I had to get the bus!'

'When?'

'When it got to half twelve and you weren't at the fucking corner!'

'Right. At half twelve I wouldn't be at any corner would I?'

'Eh? Why not? We'd arranged!'

'We arranged half eleven and you weren't there. At half twelve I was watching shitty slideshows of life achievements and saying my goodbyes.'

'What?'

'Woah, yeah, what do you mean?'

'I text this twat telling him I was already inside!'

'I thought you'd gone in to sit down!'

'No I went in because the service was starting and not a single one of you had shown up!'

'Fuck's sake!'

'No, no - we can't have missed it!'

'We can 'cos we have; that's how time works you see.'

'Don't be a dickhead!'

'Calm down, lads!'

'Is that Kev? Why the fuck is he in a bush?'

'He went for a slash that became a slush!'

'You can't do that…'

'Everyone keeps telling me that, it's disrespectful blah blah bore off!'

'No, you can't because that's the side the congregation are leaving through. I came out the front to find you spaztards!'

'What…'

'So, we've all got time to go for a drink then, yeah?'

'Aye, suppose so, Bucky.'

'Where can I leave this reef'?

Chapter 2: Pub

'What the fuck is that shit?'

As Dave carefully sets the four glasses down on the table between them, Bucky points at a bright orange liquid with an umbrella sticking up out of the glass.

'That's his!', replies Dave, visibly relieved to no longer be carrying the drink in question.

'Cookie, what the fuck is that shit?', asks Bucky again.

'It's a mocktail...I don't drink!'

'At all? Why not?', asks Mitch.

'I erm, just gave it up, you know!'

'And chose to drink blended Towie actresses instead?'

'Haha something like that.'

'So shit that we didn't say goodbye today, you know?'

'I did!'

'We know you did, Gaz!'

'Could you not have rang more of us and said it had started?'

'I could have, yeah. In fact, I'm really sorry that I didn't stop the ceremony and make a few calls. This is definitely all my fault.'

'Nobody is blaming you, mate. We're all just pissed off at ourselves!'

'I'm blaming you a bit!'

'Wanker!'

A silence settles over the table for a long second.

'Where's Kev?'

'Having a piss, I think', responds Hughesy, just sitting down with his pint.

Everyone laughs.

'Another one? I don't think I'd ever dare go to the lav again after today if I was him', says Cookie.

'It wasn't that bad, lads!', replies Kev, returning and wiping his hands on his jacket.

'You think? Grieving family members' last memories of their loved one are going to involve your homeless-looking skinny little arse curling one out!'

'Aye, it was that bad, like Kev!'

'Naw, just overreacted - especially that vicar! What a prick!'

'To be fair, I am surprised he called you a cunt!'

'Can't believe we were *all* banned from the wake. Never seen his Ma that angry!'

'Truth be told, Foz's Ma…' starts Dave.

'As much as I'd like to just discuss Kev's bowel movements, I'm gonna have to shoot for the kids soon', interjects Fat Knacker.

'Shoot on the kids, more like!'

'Vile!'

'How have you got kids, dude? Who was willing to risk their life by lying underneath you?'

'Or had the climbing experience to scale you?'

'Very funny, yeah - do you think the fat jokes can stop now after twenty-odd years?'

'No!'

'Not a chance!'

'But I'm not even fat'.

'You are on the inside!'

'And the outside.'

'You've even got a fat aura…'

'Alright, Uri Geller, don't ponce it up!'

'Lads', says Bucky, in his most serious tone of voice, 'can we just have a few moments to say a couple of words?'

Everyone falls silent again, and considers whether or not to be the one who says a couple of words. After an age, Lee clears his throat.

'Well, I guess I'll start…I still can't get my head around this at all. Like all of us, I suppose, yeah?'

Everyone nods.

'And I haven't really considered what I want to say, but I do know I miss Foz. It's weird as well, because I hadn't seen him for years, but now, knowing I can't ever see him again, feels empty and…blank…and incredibly surreal!'

'Same, mate…'

'I guess we all drifted apart but I want you to know that that never changed how much I loved you all, *love* you all, and how much I would be there for every single one of you if I had to be, if you needed me to…if he had needed…'

Gaz places a hand on Lee's shoulder, and urges him to go on.

'So, I'm saying, in a way, that I had no idea how massively I would be affected by any of this, because I'd never considered it possible. We've lost a good one, but we're here together to remember him, and give him a proper send off. To Foz…'

Everyone raises their glasses - four pints, a blended Towie actress, two waters and two cokes.

'Foz lad', in unison.

The group sit back down, and stare at the beer mats, the tiny bubbles fizzing in the coke, the TV screen showing horse racing in the corner - anywhere but at each other.

Finally, Gaz breaks the moment, saying, 'I wasn't trying to cop a feel there, mind!'

'Fucking bender', says Dave.

Lee laughs, and responds, 'No, I appreciate it mate!'

'You appreciate a bit of a fondle with a bloke? Come here then!'

'Woah, you can keep your two metres social distance, sunshine!'

As Mitch tries to grab Lee's cock, and everyone laughs, Fat Knacker stands and starts to put on his coat.

'Woah, where the fuck are you going?'

'Got to pick the kids up, haven't I!'

'What a pleb…'

'Yeah, me too I'm afraid! Traffic's murder around the school and if I'm late…'

'Fuck all will happen! I've seen your kids on Facebook; no cunt's going to try and take those two little Chucky-looking psychopaths! They'll stand around feeling abandoned for a bit, and learn a valuable life lesson that you can't rely on any fucker!'

'I wonder why you don't have kids?'

'Pull out and shoot all over the tits, don't I! You should have thought of that!', states Cookie matter-of-factly, tapping the side of his temple.

'Knacker, Hughesy, lovely seeing you in the flesh for once…shame it couldn't be under better circumstances!'

'Yeah, same lads - it is nice to see your weathered, old faces up close and filter-free for a change!'

'Let's arrange something soon, eh? I love the kids…'

'Paedo!'

'…but this is the first time I've been anywhere except dance classes and the school gates for years!'

'Are you allowed within a hundred yards?'

'Let's please just get together soon, yeah?', repeats Hughesy.

'Will do.'

'Later, lads!'

Hughesy and Fat Knacker leave, and the seven remaining friends settle back to chatting about very little.

Dave suddenly pipes up, having been watching the others for some time. 'Why hadn't you seen him for years?'

'What?' replies Lee.

'You said you hadn't seen Foz for years, but why was that? Why do you think we hadn't all stayed close? We were so tight.'

'I, for one, still am!'

Ignoring Mitch, Lee responds, 'Dave, mate, I can't get my head around this - I've no idea. I genuinely have no excuse…'

'You don't need an excuse, I'm not trying to put you on the spot - Foz and me still lived here so we saw each other quite a bit, you know. But none of us actively tried to get together with each other, did we?'

Bucky responds first, saying, 'I think it felt like we didn't need to.'

'What do you mean?', replies Cookie.

'Well, I knew you were single and probably jizzing on tits, and I knew Knacker had two kids with a proper hotty, and I know Hughesy's fucking scary bairns' names, and that Mitch split up with his woman last year and bought a car that he takes far too many pictures of and possibly shags in the exhaust. I know loads about everyone because, quite frankly, I see it online and assume that's all I need to know.'

'You're saying we saw each other online and didn't think we needed to see other offline?'

'Exactly.'

'I never saw anything online about you, Dave!'

'I'm not on social media.'

'So, what's my excuse there? I didn't know if you were okay or happy or anything…'

'I think', chimes in Mitch, 'that we assume everything *is* online. So by not seeing anything of Dave, we just forget about him.'

'Harsh!'

'I only mean in the sense of keeping up with people; not in the sense of forgetting about how much we care for each other or think about memories together!'

'Whenever I press a doorbell, I think of Dave and Foz bothering people and legging it, without telling us what they'd done.'

'I got cracked with a cane by an old bastard who came out to answer the door, and I hadn't even noticed those twats started sprinting in front of me,' adds Gaz.

'Good times!'

'Not for me! I went home with a massive welt on my head, explained to my Da what had happened, and that fucker brayed me around the other side.'

'I remember you coming into school the next day looking like a Klingon after a crash!'

'Dave, mate?'

'Yeah?'

'Sorry for not getting in touch!'

'Ah, Cookie man, it's understandable this day and age', adds Kev.

'Don't get bent, you two', responds Dave.

'Yeah, get a room, twats! You're bringing us all down!'

They all look at each other, and laugh.

'Think we're meant to be down today!'

'Sorry, kids, but I've got to get back to work. I've enjoyed this - if you can say that on a day like today.'

'You can, indeed. Sure Foz would have wanted us to have a laugh!'

'That twat would have wanted us to cause havoc.'

'True that!'

'Anyway, see you all later. Let's not leave it as long next time, eh?'

'Let's hope next time isn't for a similar reason!'

'Bloody hell, Gaz - '

'Christ, man, what a sprinkling of misery you are!'

'Sorry, I just mean I don't want to get together for another fucking funeral...where I'm the only one who turns up!'

'Let's drop that, should we?'

'Unless it's your own, you won't be the only fucker there!'

'Haha harsh again!'

Kev, walking back in the room, says 'Where are you going, you fannyfart?'

'Where am I going? Where have you been?'

'Piss.'

'Again - you've got a problem mate! I've got to get back to work!'

'Ah yeah, suppose the dog'll be going nuts cooped up!'

'You want dropping off?

'Please. Right, later boys! Been emotional to say the least! Not every day you say goodbye to one of your mates or get called a cunt by a godbotherer!

'See you later, Kev. Later, Mitch!'

'I'll just nip for a slash before we go!'

'Are you taking the piss? Actually, don't answer that...'

As Mitch leaves and Kev goes into the toilet, the barman changes the horse racing, which has finished, to the music channels. D:Ream's *Things Can Only Get Better* is mid-song.

'What a tune!'

'The year we left school this came out!'

'The year you came out', adds Dave.

'Very funny. Ironic song for today. How can things get better, eh?'

'Did they get better after school?'

'What do you mean?'

'After school; we all thought life would be fantastic and we'd all be together with mint jobs and all our lasses would be mates - didn't end up that way, did it?

'Like Lee said earlier, I guess we all drifted apart.'

'I said that?'

'In that stirring speech about misery and gloom, aye!'

'I didn't even know what I was saying, you know! I can't get my head around any of this, lads.'

'I can't believe I'll never see him again. We saw each other most days in passing, living in the same estate; I can't imagine not waving in the car, or bumping into him in the VG!'

'I suppose for you, he was still very much part of your physical life?'

'We had a pint now and then, yeah! Probably had a catch-up once every few weeks for a proper chat.'

'I saw he would post pictures with you now and then, and your other mate - that's probably another reason I felt I knew you were doing alright and didn't get in touch!'

'I guess for the rest of us, we'll just miss his online presence.'

'Getting tagged in those fucking videos that turn into loud orgasmic noises when you open them!'

'Haha yeah, or his little drunken monologues about putting the world to rights!'

'The fucking VG!'

'What?'

'You just mentioned that place, and I hadn't thought of it for years!'

'Oh, right…yeah, it's not called that anymore; it's a Happy Shopper or something.'

'Ooh I don't like that!'

'Why not?'

'Can you imagine saying you got your end away up against the Happy Shopper?'

'Might be why he's so happy!'

'Did you get laid up against the VG?'

"A lot of girls stopped being vg's behind the VG, dude!'

'Rank!'

'On that note, I have to get away.'

'Kids? Work?'

'Neither!'

'Ooh, Dave, are you under the thumb? Is it the Mrs?'

'Something like that!'

'Ah man, keep in touch will you - at least join Facebook now your middle man is no longer with us!'

'We'll have to see about that - bye for now, faggots!'

Dave leaves. A group of customers sit down at the table next to the remaining four, dragging it further away and causing a noticeable lowering of volume.

'Then there were four, eh?'

'This isn't right at all, as a send off!'

'I know what you mean!'

'Fucking four of us left, one of whom is drinking Louie Spence's jizz - it's not got the excitement Foz would have wanted.'

'Aye, it's been decent banter but four of us left by four o'clock?'

'It's embarrassing!'

'Erm, lads', whispers Gaz, 'sorry to be a further disappointment, but I have to shoot!'

'All over your Ma!'

The group on the next table glance angrily at Bucky, who has shouted that very loudly.

'Beautiful imagery, cheers. Cookie, you wanting a lift back up the crem to get the car?'

'Aye, I better - cheers!'

'Why did you leave it?'

'I thought I'd probably end up back on the drink with you lot, but it's been a quiet affair, hasn't it. See you both around.'

'Later, daters!'

'Later, maters!'

'Then there were two.'

'Bloody hell, Bucky - we need to sort this lot out!'

'I know. I was thinking, with Dave mentioning the VG…'

'…we should get everyone together for a night out like we had when we were young'uns!'

'Exactly!'

'Foz would have wanted that! Just get a couple of cans, sit on the hill in the sun, and chat shit about the old times. It would be a lovely way to see him off, and we can all get together for more than an hour!'

'Right, we'll get a message sent on Facebook for a few weeks' time so everyone can arrange it…'

'Dave's not on social media!'

'I think Gaz had his number from arranging to meet for the crem!'

'Spot on!'

'Deal - we'll give him a proper send off like he deserves!'

'Maybe it will help get my head around this as well, knowing we're doing something together! Not just handing over a scabby reef after the service, while Kev's shitting on someone's fucking remembrance garden!'

Lee

Right, twats! Saturday 22nd we are ALL meeting at the VG at 17:00. We are going to do this properly, with a few cans on the big hill in the sunshine. Foz would have wanted us all together, and we should give him the send off he deserves!

Mitch

Be there!

Cookie

Wouldn't miss it for the world. My belly butter is all over the walls of that place!

Gaz

Yeah, c u there kids

Just spoke to Dave - he'll be there as well

Hughesy

Shouldn't be a problem. Sounds like a plan.

Fat Knacker

Are we allowed in a public place there's 9 of us

Cookie

Bore off Stay Puft

Fat Knacker

Right. I'll have to check with the Mrs - she goes out with the girls on a Saturday.

Gaz

Careful that thumbprint isn't permanent!

Fat Knacker

Wanker

Bucky

We've decided you have to dress like you did in 1995 as well, cockends!

Cookie

Shit that's cruel

Hughesy

I can find a NafNaf jacket online, but has anyone got an 8-man tent to wrap around Knacker?

Kev

Sorry for the late reply, I was on the loo. I'm in!

Chapter 4: VG

Sure, the sign was now a ridiculous neon orange, with a maniacally smiling cartoon face staring helplessly out of the 'O' in Happy Shopper, but everything else about the VG was exactly the same. A decent-sized square building, made of light bricks with a flat roof, it sat with its entrance facing a sprawling tangle of ex-council houses.

However, to the left and rear of the building, which was guarded by a mess of shrubbery and trees along the left wall, lay a vast amount of open space for the centre of a modern town. Immediately to the left of the building ran a long, narrow and very shallow man-made pool of water which had never served any sort of purpose. This rectangular structure ran about a hundred and fifty feet before it was crossed by a metal bridge, and the other side dropped down to a huge, roughly oval, boating lake. The boating lake part of the water turned at a ninety degree angle and travelled about three hundred feet to the left, creating an inverted (not upside down) L-shaped border to a series of small, green hills. These hills were bordered at the front by a long, too-straight path which started at the door to the VG and travelled all the way to the next ex-council estate, crossing at the end a large wooden bridge. The sun was still high above the little hills when a large figure came over the crest of the one closest to the narrow, shallow pool of water and plonked down, facing the shop.

Lying half on his side, with one leg bent up and one elbow propping his body from the grass itself, Cookie was dressed in a bright red Kappa tracksuit that seemed to be screaming for help. He took a hip flask from his pocket, and had a swig. It was 16:53.

Squinting in the sunshine, Cookie stared at the old VG for long enough that gradually ten figures began to materialise along the wall, next to the trees, obscuring the shop itself. Cookie smiled to himself, and took another gulp.

'Fucking prick!', he mumbled.

'You're the prick!'

Cookie almost snapped Gaz in half, who hadn't expected such a violent reaction when he bent down and whispered in his ear.

'Shit, man, I didn't mean to scare you like that!'

'You didn't scare me…'

'Bloody looked like it - I thought you'd heard us coming.'

'I was…I guess I was miles away.'

'Old stomping ground, eh?'

'Yeah, I haven't been back here for years.'

'Me neither. I mean, I come home sometimes to visit people - you know, family - but I never wander the streets like we used to.'

'Would you want to?'

'Actually, yeah, I think I would!'

'Me too.'

'It was all straightforward wasn't it!'

'What - get drunk, get laid, get high, get home!'

'Haha something like that.'

'Time you make it?'

'Five.'

'Where are all these twats?'

'Well, I'm here!'

'Shitting hell, Lee - will everyone stop fucking creeping up on people?'

'I got here *with* Gaz!'

'Yeah - I said I thought you heard *us* walking up!'

'I thought you meant just you!'

'Why would I have said 'us'?'

'I've been living up Sunderland, mate; 'us' means 'I'!'

'Inbreds!'

'What were you smiling at and calling a 'prick' when we sat down then? Before Gaz put the shits up you?'

'I was just thinking about the ten of us…be nice to be all together won't it!'

'Well, minus one!'

'Ten in spirit!'

'Yeah…howay then, Lee, where is everyone - you arranged this little get together?'

'Everyone is meant to be coming! Bucky just text and he's in the VG getting some cans.'

'Knowing him, it'll be all of the cans, and bottles, and boxes of wine!'

'Na, he's matured by now!'

'Hope so…since when did any of us wear white chinos in our teenage years?'

'Gaz has already given me shit - couldn't find white jeans for blokes anywhere!'

'I'd forgotten white jeans were a thing until I met up with this paedo-looking Chino diCampo!'

'Haha.'

From the direction of the small metal bridge they heard, 'Gay boys!', and turned.'

'Dave lad, how's it going?'

'And what the fuck are you wearing?'

Dave was walking towards the group on the hill, wearing a multi-coloured tank top over a plain white t-shirt and ridiculously wide flares.

'Don't start - I ordered 90s fancy dress online and it didn't arrive until today - opened the bloody thing half an hour ago and it's fucking 70s. Thought fuck it - the lads'll appreciate the effort and at least I haven't turned up dressed like someone's perverted uncle, eh Lee?'

'I couldn't find white jeans…'

'And Gaz, you've made no effort at all! Blue jeans and a black t-shirt? How's that 90s? It's totally generic!'

'It could be from literally any decade since the fifties, to be fair Gaz!'

'So it is 90s then…and I think you've overlooked this…'

Gaz is wearing a black Casio digital watch with blue trim. It is water resistant to 50m, has a backlight and is as nineties as possible.

'Oh…fair enough mate!'

'Yeah, good job!'

'He gets more credit than I do for at least trying to wear white jeans?'

'Well, yeah definitely!'

'Here's Bucky…aw what the hell has he got?'

'Knew it!'

'And you thought he would have matured?'

Looking to their right, from around the front corner of the VG, appeared Bucky, standing still and grinning from ear to ear. Something round like the top of a bottle appeared to be in each hand, as though he were holding two bottles of wine by their necks.

'Why's the divvy just standing there?'

'He's building suspense. Fuck knows what's about to happen but it's only going to end badly.'

From behind Bucky appeared Mitch, playing an imaginary trumpet and marching. Once Mitch was in front, and had marched on the spot for a moment, they both started to walk along the long path adjacent to the shop. Revealed as he stepped away from the shelter of the building, the two bottle tops became long black poles in each of Bucky's hands, which then were attached to a silver metal wheelbarrow. This was bad enough, but the contents of the contraption were hidden from view by a blue checkered picnic blanket.

'Some bad shit is about to go down, kids!'

'What have I missed?'

'Areet, Hughesy, mate. Nice jacket! We're just thinking about doing a runner before Bucky and Mitch reveal whatever they've got in that 'barrow!'

'Ah…oh, fucking hell, I get you now. Why are they marching?'

'Not a Scooby!'

As the barrow battalion turned the ninety degree angle at the edge of the narrow pool, in order to walk straight toward the group, Kev appeared from the trees obscuring the wall of the VG.

'Please, tell me that old bastard hasn't been having another open air shite?'

'He's got issues, like!'

'I think we all have, dealing with this approaching nightmare.'

Slowly marching as they were, it didn't take long for Kev to jog around the top of the pool and catch up to Mitch and Bucky, at which point he started to play an invisible marching drum.

'Anyone seen Knacker?'

'Naw, not heard from the blimp either!'

'What time is it?'

'Quarter past five!'

'Give him time. He's got kids you know! Did you know?'

'Eeh has he?'

'Eeh, I didn't know!'

'Eeh, he hasn't ever mentioned it!'

'I've heard him mention it loads of times…'

'Okay, Gaz.'

Chapter 5: Light Whitening

'Where in this world or the next did you find Adidas Poppers?'

'Believe it or not, they're mine.'

'Yours?'

'Yeah, from 1995!'

What? Why do you still have them, Kev?'

'I just picked them up. This top as well. I told the old man we were dressing up and he said he had a load of my stuff in the attic still. I've got a box full of old crap in the boot!'

'In the boot? You haven't brought the car?'

'It's behind the VG, but don't worry, I have every intention of getting a taxi back and picking it up tomorrow...'

'...be picking it up next Thursday when you finally sober up if I have anything to do with it!' interrupted Bucky, finally dragging the wheelbarrow halfway up the hill and collapsing. Kev and Mitch had long since downed instruments and joined the others on the grass.

'Or you can pinball the thing off every car in the street imagining you're sober like Lee did back in the day!'

'I just remember thinking 'why are all these cars pulling in front of me' when it turned out there was nobody in them.'

Bucky was wearing a colour-changing t-shirt, which was a very different shade around his armpits from pulling the obviously laden wheelbarrow so far. He wore normal jeans, but had hung a chain from his belt loops.

'Kudos on the fashion choice, but in hindsight it may have been a mistake mate!' 'What...aw bollocks, that's not a good look is it?

'Not as bad as Chino Saville over there!'

'Leave it off, will ya...'

'Come on then, Bucky - what's in the wheelbarrow of death, and why's it dressed like Mitch?'

'Here, this is Ben Sherman!'

'Surprised you've not still got your Andy Cole Toon top, pal!'

'De'ath!'

'Eh?'

'Not remember Ms De'ath? She fucking hated us!'

'Oh yeah - okay, so in my 'wheelbarrow of De'ath' we have...'

Pulling back the checkered blanket, Bucky revealed a mountain of alcohol. Everything still in circulation that had existed in their youth lay on top of each other in a pile of glinting glass and colourful cans.

'...Hooch, Carlsberg Super Strength, Mad Dog 20/20, Thunderbird and the daddy of them all, White Lightning!'

'This is not good!'

'This is awesome!'

'Grab your chosen weapon and let's get started lads! In loving memory of Foz; a prick, a bastard and a wanker! We loved him for it!'

'Haha, I'll drink to that!'

'Cheers, everyone!'

'Here, where's the Fat Knacker? Don't tell me he's not been allowed to play out?'

'Prick's a cappuccino!'

'Say what?'

'He's wet *and* whipped!'

'Would you ever try to leave the house if your wife was that hot?'

'I'd try to leave my wife to get into his house!'

'Haha, I'll text the chunky fucker now.'

'I have to say, lads, looking forward to this has really helped me get my head around things - knowing we can give a proper send off to the git!'

'Yeah Lee, this feels a lot better than sitting in suits in a little pub - more fitting!'

'Even without losing Foz, I've needed this for a long time. I know that sounds...'

'Gay as fuck?' asked Dave.

'...well, yeah, but I was going to say it sounds a bit miserable, but I genuinely have missed you lot!'

'I know where you're coming from...'

'Gay again!'

'...Fuck off, you bloody homophobe. If I want to love Hughesy I will, as God is definitely not going to witness!'

'If there is one, he'll be busy a canny while trying to sort out what he's going to do with Foz!'

'Exactly. But, yeah - I know where you're coming from; we were the best group of mates I ever had, and I don't have anyone like that now!'

'Same here.'

'Agree.'

'True, yeah!'

'Pass another bottle of White Lightning mate - we had some good times, lads! This was our playground back in the day.'

'It was Gaz - we were invincible, or we felt that way!'

'Never considered any of us would be gone so soon!'

'Me neither - but life speeds up and catches up and fucks us up, doesn't it! Seems like those summers lasted for years, and every one since has flown by quicker and quicker!'

'Speaking of which, it's quarter to six and we are still just sitting still on a fucking hill...does nobody else think we need to cram as much as we can into tonight before it flies by and takes us months or years to get together again?'

'What did you have in mind? I thought sitting here and chatting shit was the point?'

'It kind of is, but actions speak louder, don't they?'

'What are you suggesting we, a group of almost-forty old men, do?'

'What we used to do!'

'Keep Cookie away from that shop wall!'

'Millions of little Cookie's already there, lads!'

'I feel a little sick!'

'Pass that picnic blanket mate!'

'What for?'

'So I can sit on it - don't want to get covered in grass stains!'

'I used...'

'We get it, man - you shagged a lot!'

'Here are Lee, next time just don't come dressed as a sex pest, eh?'

'For fuck's sake...'

'What did you have in mind, Bucky?'

'That's a dangerous question with a relatively short answer!'

'Rude!'

'Untrue?'

'Well, probably not. Me and Mitch were talking back in the VG about Foz, and that time he had us all garden hopping...'

'...but we didn't look at how many gardens were in the street, and were all fucked by the end of it!'

'Haha, you remember that bloke who was hanging his washing out...and we all landed about three feet away from him! Who was it he wiped out with the prop?'

'That would have been me', replied Gaz, pointing to a scar running from his eyebrow to where his hairline used to be.

'Gary Potter!'

'Gary Botter!', added Dave, laughing.

'Here, am I fuck playing at garden hopping mind - I'm fifteen stone of liquid muscle!'

'Same - I'm built like a shit brickhouse!'

'You mean a brick...'

'No, I know exactly what I mean!'

'Well, I'm in peak condition, dossers!'

'Alright, Kappa slapper, we can see you bash the gym nearly as much as your cock!'

'I only bash the gym a couple of hours a day, though!'

'Nice!'

The final crescendo of Queen's *Hammer To Fall* interrupted the conversation, as Fat Knacker pulled into the car park behind the VG. Waving across the narrow pond as he exited the vehicle, Knacker began walking along the tree-lined side of the shop, visibly stressed. As he turned the corner of the path at the top, the others saw him stop, hurriedly don a mask, and have a brief conversation with a younger, taller figure. He then walked around the top edge of the pond and down towards the others.

'He's not changed.'

'Same music, same waddle, same punctuality!'

'Pass another bottle of Light Whitening, lads?'

'Light Whitening?'

'That's your third litre already, Gaz!'

'Alright, Ma!'

'I'm only mortalled!'

'Bob Dylan, nice…'

'Just saying, you don't want to get so mashed we take you home by seven!'

'However mashed I get, promise not to leave me!'

'Promise, promise.'

'We used to neck them, didn't we? Don't know about you, but if I actually taste this shit I won't be drinking it at all!'

'Remember when Foz downed a three-litre bottle with blackcurrant in it, we went to that lass's house, what was she called…'

'Marie, I was seeing her', added Mitch.

'That's it, and the daft cunt spewed right there in the armchair. Cream carpet, furniture, curtains - all purple! Fucking unbelievable scenes!'

'It was like Leatherface had got a hold of Barney the Dinosaur!'

'There you go then; I'm necking this shite in loving memory of Foz, because that's what he would have wanted! Now, can someone pass me a bottle?'

Chapter 6: Knackered

'Lads!'

'Where the hell have you been?'

'Trying to find this fucking place, haven't I!'

'It's after six, did you forget what time we were meeting?'

'No, I did not fucking forget what fucking time we were fucking meeting!'

'Alright, mate - I'd offer you a drink to calm down but you've brought the…'

Knacker takes a can of Super Strength out of the wheelbarrow.

'We were starting to think that the woman had grounded you?'

'Ah, that's better. Still absolutely vile after twenty-odd years but better! Right, first things first - why the shitting hell is he dressed as Gary Glitter?'

'They're chinos lads, get over it!'

'I don't recall the dress code being 'dangerous flasher'!'

'I don't recall the arrival time being 'an hour late because I was chasing the Greggs delivery van'!'

'Shots fired!'

'Shots needed?' Hughesy pulled a bottle of Aftershock from his NafNaf jacket.

'So, I've been driving around since four o'clock trying to find the 'VG' on the satnav. Get here and it's a Happy Shopper, man! Who knew?'

'We all did, didn't we? Talked about it in the pub the other week.'

'I didn't hear that!'

'Ah, you and Hughesy left early doors didn't you?'

'Sorry, man - didn't think to put that in the message!'

'I was meant to text you and see where you were half an hour ago, but I got sidetracked helping this one avoid Operation Yewtree!'

'Wait…surely you remembered where this place was? We spent every Friday and Saturday night here for about three years.'

'I lived that way!' Gesturing towards the second ex-council estate, at the end of the very long path and over the large wooden bridge, Knacker started to lighten up. 'I never knew how to get here by road!'

'Haha you useless twat! Why didn't you ring?'

'I tried Gaz but his phone just kept going to voicemail. I don't think I have any other numbers and I can't get on Facebook on this brick!' Knacker holds up his Nokia 3210.

'Jesus, is that your 90s dress-up?'

'Good one. Came out in the noughties, pal! You're dressed as someone who didn't bother to do fancy dress in the last eight decades.'

'Casio classic mate!'

'Oh…fair enough! Naw, if I have a flashy phone the kids just use it to watch Peppa or Paw Patrol or something. Better off left alone with this.'

'But you can't do anything with it, either!'

'Yeah, but I don't have to watch kids' TV…in fact, they don't even come to find me so I can just have some peace and quiet!'

'Seems like a good plan!'

'And I can play Snake!'

'Don't get Cookie started!'

'Why've you brought a mask?'

'I'm 'clinically extremely vulnerable…'

'You're clinically extremely inflatable!'

'Wonderful...so I'm meant to be shielding.'

'But we're outdoors!'

'And even if we stood at your belly button we'd be two meters from your face!'

'Not for the germs, unless I intend to get close to people...so the police can't recognise me!'

'I think they will 'a' have no problem recognising a Jerry Springer special, and 'b' have no bother at all catching up to you.'

'What is your dress code, then?'

'I figured you'd all expect me to come as a tent or a blimp or some other hilarious fat joke, so I've come as the opposite!'

Fat Knacker removed his black hoody and grey joggers, revealing bright green shorts and vest.'

'What the fucking arsing hell is that?'

'Mr. Motivator, aren't I!'

'Mr. Roastpotator!'

'We said to dress *as* we dressed, not to dress *up*.'

'Eh, I thought it was fancy dress! Dave's in fancy dress!'

'Just a mix-up on the ordering mate.'

'Well, at least there's three of us look like twats!'

'Who's the third?'

'Man from Del Monte over there!'

'I'll take that; at least it's not a suggestion that I'm a predator.'

'Good job you've got that mask so you don't stand out, mate!'

'Knacker lad, who were you talking to over there?'

'Where? Oh, some little scrote asking me to go in the shop for him and his mates.'

'Nothing changes, does it?'

'That was us, harassing people all the time. Going out to buy a loaf of bread and ending up with a box of cider and forty fags.'

'Where would we have been without morally irresponsible adults, eh?'

'Looking back, for a lot of them, it was probably self-preservation.'

'What do you mean?'

'We weren't nasty or bullies like you see young'uns acting now, but I bet people thought we could have been if they'd not done us the favour.'

'So how come you didn't go in?'

'What?'

'For the lad - why didn't you help him out like we always asked of people?'

'You know, if I wasn't running so late and so pissed off already, I might have! I probably should have been politer to be honest.'

'Why, what did you say to him?'

'I told him to go fuck himself...'

'That's not too bad!'

'...once he'd finished fucking his Ma.'

'Woah, Knacker - brutal!'

'As brutal as some bloke on a bike calling me a 'fat knacker' when we were twelve and then everyone forgetting my real name?'

'What is your real name?'

'It's...'

'No no no - we don't want to hear it! Knowing your actual name would destroy my childhood memories, like if we found out Gaz was really a genius or Lee wasn't on a register!'

'Haha, you fucking chinophile!'

'I am really regretting my effort!'

'Anyway, what have I missed so far?'

'We were talking about the old days and the old tricks - Bucky and Mitch think we should cause some havoc and...'

'I'm up for that as well!'

'Me too!'

'...Okay, so Bucky, Mitch, Cookie and Gaz all think we, as fully grown, responsible humans, should tear shit up.'

'Yeah, count me in!'

'Knacker, lad, get in! Hughesy? Dave? Leedophile?'

'Leedophile is actually clever! I'm game for a laugh!'

'Count me in, then!'

'Don't wanna let the side down!'

'So, literally every one of you want to act like irresponsible teenagers?' The entire group nod and smile at Kev.

'Fuck it then, let's do it! I've got some stuff in the car!'

'That your car next to mine over there?'

'Yeah!'

'So those are your...'

'Don't spoil the surprise! I've picked a few things up at my Da's on the way here!

'Right, drink up and we'll start over to Kev's car then, lads! Throw all the empties in the 'barrow!'

'Not too irresponsible I see!'

'We're still humans. We just want to have some fun. And irritate people.'

The group collect their empties and pile them into the wheelbarrow as Bucky secures the blanket over the top of them to hold them in place. As he stands up, Gaz wobbles on his feet and Lee steadies him, before noticing a tiny green stain on his chinos. Licking his thumb and rubbing at it doesn't make much of a difference. Upon looking up, Lee realises that the group have started to head towards the car park without him, and begins walking to catch up, still focusing on his trousers.

'Right, I'm going for a slash!'

'Where?'

'Trees - wall - old school!'

'Have you got a problem down there, Kev? You can tell us!'

'Piss off! I've just had half a bottle of cider for the first time in two decades! I'll be back!'

'Anyone want anything in the VG?'

'I need some fags!'

'Bet you do!', smirked Dave.

'I'm gonna get some cordial and Foz this pissy water right up - fuck up some cream curtains!'

'Yeah, I'll come along - could do with some ket!'

'Not that type of shop!'

'Lads, I'm going to start dragging this thing along to the boathouse; catch me up! Mitch, you coming?'

'Yeah I'll help Titsmarch here!'

'Knacker, you coming in?', asked Dave.

'I'll just wait here.'

'Want out?'

'I'm good, cheers! Had a big dinner before I left the house.'

'No bother…'

'Actually go on…I'll have a big bag of Doritos, a packet of custard creams, a two-litre bottle of Irn Bru, a multi-pack of Snickers and er...a whole roast chicken if they've got one of those hot food counters!'

'Right.'

'Make it diet Irn Bru!'

Leaning back against the light brickwork at the front of the shop, facing towards the ex-council houses, Fat Knacker faintly began to see ten figures walking in a huddle along the path towards the shop door. Squinting in the evening sunlight, he could only make out one face, and that was Foz - gesturing wildly and clearly telling a story the others found hilarious, as the shadows kept separating and roaring with laughter before coming back together for another instalment. With barely a breeze, and the heat penetrating his face, he began to hear the story in front of him as a memory long forgotten. A slight smile began to spread across his face.

'That's the cunt there!'
'This fat, old fucker?'
'Aye!'
'Here, pal?'
Fat Knacker came out of his trance instantly. Before him, and where he had been staring at his own group of friends from the past, were six teenage boys and a girl. Their expressions were not those of a group who are out enjoying a tall tale from one of their members.
'What? Me?'
'Yeah - you tell my boy here to fuck our Mam?'
'Sorry? Oh him, no!'
'You calling him a liar, like hew?'
'How what?'
'Eh?'
'How what?'
'I said hew!'
'What does that mean?'
'It's like…it doesn't fucking matter! Are you calling him a liar?'
'Yes, absolutely!'
'Nar, you fucking said that!'
'Don't be a pussy you old twat!'
'I'm not being a pussy, I'm telling you I did not tell him to fuck his Ma! I told him to fuck off when he was through *already* fucking her!'

'See - fucking do him, Sean!'

The eldest of the group, and most sizeable, grabbed Fat Knacker by the front of his bright green vest as Knacker frantically tried to get his mask on.

'Listen here…'

'No, you listen here, son…' interrupted Lee, as he arrived along the side of the shop. 'Take your hands off my mate, and piss off!

'We better run, like…he's dressed as a paedo!'

'Haha you want some as well, eh Grandad?'

Three of the other boys turned on Lee, who stood perfectly still, while Sean and the two brothers kept their attention on Fat Knacker.

'Go on, lads - kick their fucking faces in!'

'She's classy, isn't she!'

'Shut your fucking mouth, paedo cunt!'

'They're chinos you scabby little rat! Fucking come on then!'

At this, Sean smashed his fist into the side of Fat Knacker's cheek, causing him to fall sideways. Lee jumped forward and landed clean shots on two of the boys before the third jumped on his back. As Fat Knacker looked up from the floor, smelling faeces and hoping he hadn't soiled himself, reeling from kicks to his stomach and back, he saw the giant frame of Sean suddenly plucked from view. Hesitating with their talisman missing for a split second, Fat Knacker grabbed the leg of the younger brother (the one who had asked him to go into the shop earlier) and pulled his balance out from under him. With this reprieve, he staggered to his feet.

About ten feet away, Lee and Dave were shouting at four of the boys to keep running, or something along those lines. To their right, squashed up against the side of a house with blood running from his nose, was Sean. Squashing him: Cookie.

Holding his arm up his back and pushing his face against the wall, Cookie was saying something in Sean's ear before releasing him, and watching him run away after the others. To the left of all of this, Gaz was struggling to pour blackcurrant cordial into a White Lightning bottle.

Chapter 7: Tribute

Leaving the shop with an armful of sweets, Hughesy stopped and stared at the scene in front of him.

'What the fuck has happened here?'

'Where were you?'

'In the VG. I was two people behind you in the queue and you didn't look like that then!'

'Like what?' Dave looked down at his now-bloodied tank top. 'Bollocks!'

'Ah, shite! I've got blood on me, man!' shouted Lee, looking at an indistinct area of his right leg while Dave, next to him, looked like a scene from Carrie.

'And your face wasn't like that when we left you, Knacker!'

'Gang of little shits, man! 'Cos I didn't buy their drink earlier!'

'Really?'

'Well, and because of the incestuous comment! Didn't expect this lot to turn up though, did they?'

'The look on that big lad's face when Cookie grabbed him, man! Classic!'

'I think one of them shit themselves! Literally, I mean!'

'That was me!', responded Kev, stepping out from the trees at the side of the shop.

'Thought you went for a whizz!'

'I did. It turned. I tried snapping it off when I heard Dangerpants shout 'come on then', but it was free-flowing!'

'So I was getting kicked *to* shit *and* inhaling it at the same time?'

'Yeah, sorry!'

'You stink, dude!'

'That's better! Can't even tell now!'

'Lee, I look like a Rob Zombie film and you're bothered about your creepy uncle's trousers!

'You know what - I know we were up for causing trouble but I actually don't fancy the police coming along to arrest me for beating up adolescents and drinking on the streets, so can we make a move?'

'Yeah, let's catch up with the Wheelbarrow of Doom.'

Walking together around the shop, Kev quickly grabbed a couple of things from his car, stuffed them into a small backpack, and threw Dave's tank top into the back seat. Similarly, Fat Knacker disposed of his hoody and joggers, claiming it was too hot to put them back on. As they walked around the outer perimeter of the boating lake, passing the little metal bridge, they soon saw Bucky and Mitch sitting where the boats were always launched from in the Summer holidays. Behind them, however, stood no boathouse.

'Another change!'

'Things can't stay the same.'

'Why not?'

'Stagnant, isn't it!'

'Looks to me like they made changes 'round here and things are still stagnant!'

'Don't know if you're being profoundly philosophical or ridiculously literal!'

'I have not a clue what either of those means!', replied Gaz.

'Let's go literal, then!'

'Lads, you've lost the boathouse!'

'We have, aye! Feels like part of our childhood has been torn away!'

'More space for us all to have a chinwag, eh?'

'Alright, Nana!'

'Do you have biscuits for us during this chinwag?'

'Actually, I do! Dave, where's my snacks?'

'Bollocks, sorry mate. I must have dropped the bag when I came out of the shop and saw what was going on!'

'Wait, what the hell happened to you lot? We only left you ten minutes ago!'

'Wey, Knacker got a crack off a smackhead, Lee went full Bez, and then Cookie wrestled a gorilla. But the biggest achievement was Gaz getting cordial into a bottle!'

'That's a canny black eye, mate!'

'Hurts like fuck - got a right stitch in me side as well!'

'Did you have to run a metre?

'Piss off!'

'Who was it?'

'Little chav prick Knacker told to fuck his Ma…'

'I told him to *finish* fucking her, if you want to be accurate!'

'…yeah, well he turned up with his little gang of street rats and tried to intimidate Knacker, didn't he!'

'He wasn't expecting us though!'

'To be fair, I was definitely still very much intimidated!'

'Understandable!'

'But I'll be okay.'

'My clothes won't be!'

'Ooh, bet you're regretting the ridiculous t-shirt now!'

'I wasn't being…yeah, ridiculous I guess!'

'So while we've been going fully Green Street, what have you two been up to?'

'We've been concocting!'

'Drinks?'

'Plans!'

'I'm going to regret this, but please - do go on.'

The group formed a rough semi-circle sitting on the paved slabs where the boathouse once stood; Lee positioned the picnic blanket and sat down, giving the white chinos one more check over. At the semi-circle's centre sat Bucky, as a kind of honorary leader. The others opened their drinks, took in the still-warming sun, and then one by one looked toward him.

'A tribute', Bucky began, his back to the water, before tailing off and looking toward a path running diagonally off to the right, between a primary school railing and some houses.

'That's where Foz would appear, right?' asked Dave.

'Yeah, exactly. I've caught myself glancing over there a few times already, expecting to see him materialise with his Aldi carrier bag…'

'I forgot about that!'

'He used to help his Ma shopping to get bottles didn't he! Bloody hell!'

'…with that bag and his stupid grin on his face! That bouncy way he walked - you can see that path from where we sat over there as well, and from the corner of the VG! He was the one of us who you never missed coming, and who never missed where we were at the start of the night.'

'That was a right arse on - before mobiles. From the Monday we'd be saying to everyone 'VG at five on Friday' and there'd still be one turn up the next Monday saying 'where were you lot Friday - I was at the VG at seven!'

The group all looked toward Fat Knacker.

'Yeah, that was me - and if you missed Friday you couldn't possibly know where to go for Saturday!'

'I would ring Foz the Saturday morning during SM:TV even if I'd been there on the Friday, 'cos he'd always know where we were meeting!'

'Same - I knew his landline off by heart...what was it again? Three double...'

'...one, double oh one', the others all chanted in unison.

'Fuck, I miss him!'

'I'm just starting to get my head around the fact that he's gone.'

'It's nice that you've developed a catchphrase, Leedo!'

Bucky started up again, focused on the pile of drink in the wheelbarrow and avoiding the path to the right and the eyes of the other eight grown men dressed like Byker Grove extras.

'A tribute, lads, is only truly a tribute if it in some way represents the person you are paying tribute to! Foz liked to drink awful vinegary-tasting piss - check. Foz liked to spend time with the boys - check. Foz liked to skirt trouble - check already for you lot. Foz loved - *LOVED* - bothering people!'

'Oh no...'

'So, with immediate effect...'

'Ah, I see where we're going with this...'

'I don't...'

'...I declare the Foz Tribute Nicky Nocky Nine Doors Open Tournament officially afoot!'

'Shit!'

'Yes! Get in.'

'We're a bit old for that, lads, howay!'

'Hey, no dissension in the ranks! Bucky and me's thought this through!', chimed in Mitch, looking the most normal alongside Gaz in his Ben Sherman shirt.

'I really doubt it, but do go on!'

'Mitch is right - we take our fun very seriously for the benefit of our troops!'

'Okay, there's obviously no point fighting this.'

'So, there are a number of rules for the Foz Tribute Nicky Nocky Nine Doors Open Tournament, that should be followed at all times. Rule number one - we are all older and unhealthier so we pick one house each and that's it. We aren't legging it all over the place! Numero two - you have to give the rest of us a head's up before you knock…no surprises! We don't want Gaz taking a cane to the face. Finally, number drei - if you're stupid enough to get caught, we leave you.'

'Woah the army analogy ended pretty abruptly - what about leave no man behind?'

'Let's be honest - and we can be, this is a safe space - we probably won't get together again like this for another decade or two, so are we fuck ruining our night for one prick who can't play a kid's game properly!'

'Harsh, but fair!'

'We all know this is aimed at me, right?'

'Knacker, mate - we all are very aware that this is aimed at you, yes!'

'Fuck's sake - pass me another bottle of that Mad Dog, and can I borrow some blackcurrant Gaz?'

'Gaz, Knacker wants some…'

'Spanner's asleep!'

'Anyone think he does need a cane to the face?'

'What a sack of shit! I'm not carrying him around all night!'

'Leave him here!'

'He actually made us promise to look after him.'

'Empty the wheelbarrow!'

'Haha great idea - okay, so once we leave the confines of the boating lake, it's game on! If we have to run, two people need to take a handle each of this daft cunt, and remember the rules!'

Chapter 8: One Door

From the position of the old boathouse, which was behind and to the left of the VG, the group began to walk further to the left. Following the path, with the boating lake on their left and the primary school fence on their right, they came to a small wooden bridge, one of many among these estates that criss-crossed the narrow beck that ran through the town. It took three of them to push the wheelbarrow over the hump of the bridge, as not only did it contain a comatosed Gaz, but also a still-hefty amount of alcohol. Marking their exit from the relative safety and maturity of the boating lake and its surrounding hills and grassy areas, the bridge was crossed by a group whose expressions ranged from sheer joy and excitement, to abstract despair at the task ahead. At the rear of the group, Dave and Kev were talking.

'I'll forget about my jumper!'

'I'll forget whose it was or why it was covered in blood and have to admit to the family that I possibly may have murdered a Blue Peter presenter!'

'Well, let's hope I don't forget it, then!'

'At least you had your Spice Girls t-shirt on underneath - some lengths you've gone to with the dressing up! Nineties undergarments weren't on my list. I would have worn my Vengaboys boxers had I planned as well as you have."

'I literally just threw it on - it was the first one in the drawer.'

'Wife's, eh?'

"Well, no..."

'How come you didn't tell us all that the boathouse was gone?'

'You're the only person to notice that. I saw the expressions in the pub when I said the VG was a Happy Shopper - I couldn't be responsible for destroying any more memories!'

'I appreciate your tact!'

'Do you think this is a good idea?'

'No - I think a Boyzone top would have been better!'

'Piss off - *this*!' Dave gestured at the group ahead of them. 'Should a group of late thirties blokes be wandering around, drinking and planning to cause mayhem?'

'It's Knock Door Neighbour, man - what can possibly cause havoc with that? We'll inconvenience a few people, feel like we're wild and young again for a split second - nothing untoward will happen!'

'Knock Thy Neighbour? What the fuck?'

'Knock *Door* Neighbour! Unless you're posh!'

'Who calls it that?'

'I dunno, I must have heard it somewhere!'

'Downton Abbey?'

'It's Knock Door Ginger down Brighton…'

'That's just racist!'

'Alright, Knock Door Run, then!'

'Lads…lads! Has anyone else ever called Nicky Nocky Nine Doors 'Knock Thy Neighbour' or 'Knock Door Run'?'

'Oh yeah! I do…'

'See?'

'…when I'm not calling it 'Tap Tap Run Away'!'

'I prefer the classic 'Press a Doorbell, Leg It Fast'!'

'Okay, you bunch of pricks - Nicky Nocky; happy?'

'Bucky would have called it 'Bang Door Punch A Dick', wouldn't you, mate!'

'Why the hell did you go and bring…'

'I absolutely *would*! Yes, I *would*! I had almost forgotten about *that*! Right, I'm going first, boys!'

Bucky began surveying the estate in front of him as Kev and Dave came off the bridge. Around the wheelbarrow Fat Knacker, Lee and Mitch were breathing heavily as Gaz started to snore gently.

'What you looking for, Bucky?'

'This is an art form, Hughesy. You can't rush into these things. Given the precise nature of the task in hand, or balls in hand if you prefer, I have to be sure of my target!'

'Meaning…'

'Meaning that when I ring the bell, and the silhouette appears at the door, and I shoot my hand through the letterbox and give them the fright of their cock, I cannot under *any* circumstances, and I emphasise this, grab a handful of fanny flaps!'

'He's gone there!'

'Aw, mate - yeah, I see your point. There's a difference between harmless pranks and sexual assault!'

'Is there though?' asked Cookie. 'Male or female, I'd say you're committing the same assault!'

'No, and besides it's just a prank!'

'That is an excuse that may have worked in our teens, but what are you going to say to the judge in your late thirties? I was just testing letterboxes for a career change to be a postman?'

'The judge, man! Howay, stop being a ray of cloudshine!'

'That makes no sense.'

'I make no sense!'

'On that we agree!'

'Anyway, Hughesy, as I was saying…to be sure of the target, you have to look at the details. See this house here? That's a no-go!'

'Why?'

'Pink curtains at the top right window and a car seat in the back of the Passat!'

'Could be separated - could have his kid on a Friday not a Saturday!'

'Wrong.'

'How?'

'Three ways - first, if the kid doesn't live there then those curtains are generically coloured and a few teddies get thrown on the bed on the day it stays over! Second, the car seat would not be on show if that were a single man, as it would be in the boot unless needed.'

'Interesting, but he may be a single dad with custody!'

'Can't be.'

'Why not?'

'He has a Passat! Who the fuck buys a Passat? The elderly and the men who have a woman making their decisions! That's it!'

'He has made a good argument there, like.'

'Now this house is perfect', continued Bucky. 'You see how the guy has a pick-up truck that has been waxed - excess cash like Mitch with his car porn.'

'It's not car porn, lads - it's a hobby!'

'It's a replacement wife - you wank the gearstick!'

'My wife didn't have a cock!'

'Bet she's getting plenty now!'

'You what?'

'And there's nothing on any of the windowsills!'

'Sorry?'

'Women put candles or ornaments of angels on windowsills, don't they! He lives alone!'

'Hughesy san, you learn fast!'

'So now what?'

'Now I go flick-the-dick and we scarper! Rule two - I am making you all aware that I am about to Nicky Nocky!'

As the rest of the group moved to the corner of the estate, so that they could see Bucky's target letterbox between the garage and the position of the truck, Bucky himself edged closer to the door.

'This is going to be brilliant!'

'Hope so. Don't think we should be encouraging this!'

'Ah, it'll be fine mate!'

By now, Bucky was crouched down next to the letterbox, with the flap open to listen. 'He's checking for a dog!'

'Bloody hell, he's thought of everything hasn't he!'

'He's an artiste!'

Looking back toward the group, Bucky removed his watch and glanced at the time, causing Fat Knacker to look at his own (the way a yawn makes others yawn) and inform the group that it was ten past seven. He gave a thumbs up and then reached up to press the doorbell. Lifting the flap again, he positioned his hand just inside the letterbox, fingertips against the inner flap. From where the group watched in anticipation, they saw a rectangle light up on the front of the door, and the emergence of a shadowy figure through the distorted glass. Just as the handle began to move, Bucky thrust his hand forward into the house.

Chapter 9: Two Doors

'Well, I bet he's regretting that whole 'leave people behind' speech, now!'

'Like he said, he'll catch up soon enough.'

'Yeah, give him ten minutes and he'll be back with us by half past!'

'We just waiting for him or we continuing the game?'

'He's the one who said we weren't letting useless twats spoil our fun!'

'Fuck it, then! I'm knocking lads! Fair warn!'

'Guessing you're not an artiste, Mitch?'

'Am I fuck - ready?'

Mitch began to walk up the path toward the first front door he came to, as the others sped up a little. As he neared the door itself, a figure came to close the curtains on the large bay window at the front of the property. Mitch, rather than ducking out of sight, walked straight over to the window and tapped on the glass just as the curtains were drawn.

'What the fuck is the walking picnic blanket doing?'

'Not. A. Scooby!'

'Christ!'

The curtains opened a little, and a face the group could barely make out peered back at Mitch. The curtains closed and after a second or two, the front door opened.

'Mitch is playing 'Knock Knock Can I Come In For Tea' by the looks of things!'

'What is he actually playing at?'

'These two came up with the plan and are completely fucking this up!'

After a brief conversation, Mitch waved the lads away and stepped into the house, the door closing behind him.

'Fuck.'

'He's messaged in the group!'

'What's he say?'

'It's only Marie's house isn't it. I'll catch up in a minute!'

Chapter 10: Three Doors

'Well, that's two down already. This is going well!'

'Mitch is just checking out her clean curtains, and Bucky can't be much longer!'

'Bet he is!'

'Here, one of you take this sleeping retard, will you?'

Cookie handed over the wheelbarrow and it took both Fat Knacker and Hughesy to lift it. He removed a can of Hooch out of the side, and stretched. A few streets away they heard the sound of approaching sirens.

Dave came jogging along to catch up with the group.

'Where've you been? We can't lose more people!'

'Did my knock, didn't I!'

'Where? When? You didn't tell us, man!'

'It just seemed like as good a chance as any - sorry, I didn't think. Rules *are* rules though!'

'We've got the rules 'cos you and Foz always stitched people up!'

'Literal stitches for sleeping cutie, here!'

'I take it you're not getting caught!'

'No chance. You're not going to drink that shite are ya?'

'Aye!'

'Thought you'd quit drinking?'

'I have.'

'Tell that to that hip flask we saw when we were walking up to meet you!'

'Well, I *had*.'

'Why, anyway? You never said in the pub?'

'I have a...temper problem, sometimes, I suppose...'

'So will I if you drink all my Hooch!

'What?'

'I text Bucky and asked him to specifically get me Hooch!'

'Howay, I only like fruity alcopops and that!'

'Fucking hell, that chick drink in the pub wasn't a joke?'

'Hell no - got to keep it sweet!'

'I'll just have this one - for the memories! It doesn't look right on you anyway!'

'Don't judge a book by its cover!'

'Actually, I reckon you should never judge a book by its cover, unless it is in fact a fucking book!'

'Eh?'

'The cover is specifically designed to represent the contents, so you are meant to make a judgment based on the cover! That's the complete purpose of a cover, is it not?'

'Put like that…'

'However you want to choose reading material doesn't have any relevance to what drink I choose to drink!'

'Look, if you're the type of guy who likes an alcopop or a cocktail or the occasional finger up…'

'Fuck you, you little wanker! Am I fuck gay!'

'I wasn't trying to pick...'

'Well, it seemed like you were trying to be clever, or maybe suggest something, Dave!'

'I don't think *you're* gay.'

'Good. I'm more of a man than any of you little pussies. That big twat back at the shop can vouch for that. In fact, here's your warning that I'm knocking on a door!'

'Which one?'

'I literally don't care. What the fuck are they going to do if they open up and *I'm* slowly walking off down the path? Do you think anyone's going to try and stop *me*? Or have a pop? No chance!'

As the others reeled from Cookie's sudden anger, he started to walk down a private road. The gates were open, and there were about seven houses on each side, facing each other, all with high hedges separating them from one another and obscuring the views to any of the doorways.

'Well, that was a bit much!'

'It's still a difficult time for all of us; I mean, I haven't got my head around it yet myself', replied Lee. 'Give him a minute to calm down.'

'Message from Mitch: 'Soz lads, gonna stay for a cuppa, not be long like'. To be fair, he spent most of year eleven with her rather than us! Until Foz happened and they split up!'

'Is that why they split up? Hardly Mitch's fault, if you ask me!'

'I think she was just banned from all social life forever.'

'Ah, now that does seem fair if you turn your parents' living room into smelly modern art!'

'Haha - what time did he send that?'

'Twenty five to eight. Just now, really!'

'Well, let's knock around here a bit, then double back to meet up with him.'

'And check on Bucky?'

'Yeah, suppose we better.'

'Anyone see where Cookie went?'

'Hadn't noticed - one of those about halfway down probably.'

As the others continued to discuss Bucky's unusual predicament, Cookie was slowly walking through an overgrown garden, muttering to himself about how he should control his temper in front of his friends. A few steps from the front door, he became acutely aware that the breeze was no longer carrying their voices, and all was silent. In no rush whatsoever, he mounted the four steps up to the old, wooden door, and depressed the doorbell.

As Cookie's finger pushed the metal disc inward, his gigantic frame was thrown backwards, across the steps and into the long, overgrown tangle of grass and weeds. Before he felt his back hit the ground, his senses failed him.

'Well, unless he's done a Bucky - which I don't see happening with those arms - or bumped into an ex, which is possible at every house in town for Cookie, I think we've lost another one!'

'Pissing hell; let's have a wander down and see where he is then?'

'Someone give me a hand with this gimp?'

'Yeah, I will!'

'Cheers, dude.'

As Lee and Dave lifted the contraption, the remaining members of the group started to walk along the private road. Looking right and left in each garden as they went, they saw pristine lawns, children's play equipment, overgrown jungles, paved patios and definitely no giant angry man. Reaching the entrance to the private road at the far end, Hughesy turned to the others as if he had just made some amazing discovery.

'I know where he is!'

'Where?'

'Look over there', gestured Hughesy, grinning.

Beyond the far end of the road they were now leaving, a steep hill rose up toward a white, wooden fence, beyond which towered a whiter stone structure.

'Is that…'

'It's the…'

'…cem!'

'No way. How are we even here? It used to take forever to get up there.'

'Yeah, but we always followed the road around to it.'

'I still never liked going up there!', mumbled Knacker.

'It hadn't even started being used for burials yet, back in the day!'

'Just the idea of hanging out in a cemetery - it freaked me out. I don't know how many times I whitied because of that.'

'You whitied because you're a puff', said Dave, smirking.

'You may need to stop calling people gay!

'I can handle my ganja, I will have you know!'

'Ganja! Fucking hell, I haven't heard it called that for years!'

'Says the guy saying things like 'pleb' and 'spanner'!
'Haha touché!'
'We having some dope, lads?'
'Gaz - as if that's what wakes you up!'
'Once a stoner, always a stoner.'
'To be honest, I never stopped. Will someone help me the fuck out of this thing?'

As Dave held the wheelbarrow still for Gaz to be pulled out by Lee, he staggered to his feet again.

'You okay?'

'Yeah - I've not been sleeping since…you know. Just stay up watching horror films all night. You were all talking and the sun was on my face by the boaty - for a few seconds I could see Foz with us and we were all young again, then I'm here. In gardening equipment. Covered in booze.'

'Like Ollie Reed in B&Q!'

'You were flat out, mate.'

'Have you lot pushed me all the way to the cemetery?'

'A lot has happened, but no we didn't go on that walk. We think Cookie's gone ahead up there so we're climbing up, and thankfully you woke up just in time to not need carrying.'

If Cookie's up there, where's Bucky and - who else is missing - Mitch?'

'Well, Mitch is having a 'cup of tea' with Marie, and Bucky is…we'll show you if he hasn't caught up soon.'

Together the six of them climbed the side of the hill, and left the wheelbarrow by the edge of the fence, out of sight from the path below, before scaling it. Last to climb, Hughesy passed a six-pack of Ace lager over to Lee, before joining them. They all automatically turned right at the stone building and walked to a series of wooden benches overlooking the town.

'No Cookie.'

'Bizarre. We'll have a look back along that road on the way back.'

'Let's have a seat a minute though, can we?'

'You only climbed a hill!'

'And a fence…I'm not in good shape!'

'You are, but the shape is oval!'

'Knacker, I'm not gonna lie, but there was a moment when you jumped down from the fence, in your awful outfit, and I thought I was watching a cheap reboot of Ghostbusters!'

'Ha fucking ha!'

'We all find it funny!'

'I didn't get it?', added Gaz, as the others continued to chuckle.

The daylight was beginning to fade, and some of the warmth leaving the air, as they sat down and stared out at the town below them.

'Fucking Ace?'

'Nineties classic.'

'It would be this or those tiny bottles of beer, like ten for two quid, in a little cardboard case (remember them?) - that wins the shittest lager of the lifetime award.'

'Me Da always took them camping…Biere something?'

'I think that's just foreign for lager!'

'Or beer, perhaps?'

'You know what I mean. This is beautiful, up here. Is Foz scattered here, do we know?' asked Fat Knacker, barely recovering from climbing the hill and the fence.

'I don't actually know.'

'Me neither.'

'He liked it up here - we all did, except you, Knacker, who apparently thought the ghosts moved in before the dead bodies!'

'Fuck you.'

'We need to open up more, you know?'

'I'll open you up!'

'I'm serious...we're like, closed doors sometimes, if you get the metaphor.'

'Simile!'

'Come on, we're getting the Saved By The Bell meaningful message here!'

'Sorry, but it's the only thing I ever concentrated on in English!'

'We all could do with just being nice to each other and saying what we really think and really feel, and helping each other.'

'I really do think 'fuck you' a lot!'

'Let's just start opening the doors, yeah?'

Silence settled.

'You know what I loved the most up here like lads?' asked Gaz eventually.

'What, pal?'

'I don't recall if it was a Friday or a Saturday, or what time it happened or anything…'

'Shit, we don't need your detailed in-depth life story!'

Gaz continued, oblivious of the sarcasm, '…but we'd be sat here wasted, and then all of the lights below would start flashing like the whole town was a rave!'

'Ah shit yeah - Don't Forget Your Toothbrush!'

'Awesome. Pick n' mix anyone?', offered Hughesy.

'Cheers.'

'Did people have to flick their lights on and off and someone would knock on their door to win prizes or something?'

'Yeah, that's it! But to see it happening all at the same time - now that was something else!'

'Wouldn't happen nowadays!'

'What you mean?'

'Well, some cunt would complain that they blew their bulbs and want compensating, and half the people would be watching it on delay or catch-up the next day or have it paused - it just wouldn't happen like it used to.'

'The simple things, eh? We were privileged to a life without flash forward or flashback - the last generation of kids to not have mobiles and photographic evidence of everything we did. We didn't have to worry about CCTV catching us in the act or school texting home!'

'Too right - they sent a letter home every week for me but I left the house after me Ma and got home before her, so I binned the lot.'

'We also missed meeting up half the time!'

'Only you, Knacker son. Only you. Nowadays, everyone has an excuse to be late as well though, don't they. They can just send a text and rock up quarter of an hour later. Ruined punctuality, technology has!'

'And adventure - we used to drive all over for the craic when we got to college but then satnavs came along and you knew where you were going and the best route to get there and back. Getting lost used to be fun.'

'Not for me tonight!'

'Eh?'

'If I hadn't been lost and late I never would have got us into bother!'

'Ah don't worry about that - it's over and done with!'

'Still, without technology this last year would have been much worse - no working remotely and all that!'

'Pleasant as it is setting the failings of the modern world to rights, I think we should head back and find these three twats!'

'Hey up, Chinostradamus has prophesied it is time to move!'

Chapter 12: Door Three

By quarter past eight the group had scaled back over the fence, retrieved the wheelbarrow and come back down the hill. Splitting into three pairs, Fat Knacker and Hughesy pulled the wheelbarrow along the gated road while Lee and Dave checked alternating houses on the right hand side and Gaz and Kev checked the other. The group reconvened at the top end of the road, just outside the gates.

'No sign?'

'Nope.'

'How do you lose a giant?'

'Dunno, but we have!'

'Kev, you've been quiet a while!'

'Bursting lads, but you can't piss in a cemetery can you!'

'Water the flowers.'

'Nice.'

'I'll be back in a minute…'

'Nobody'd seen him that I spoke to'

'Same yeah - and you'd remember that at your door, dressed head to foot in bright red Kappa!'

'There was a little old lady, bless her - sure she was someone's Nana from school, really recognised her - asked if I'd like to come in. Poor thing.'

'Sad that, when they're that lonely!'

'That they'd invite a paedo in?'

'That's enough with the pants now, eh?'

'No chance.'

'Yeah, she said nobody had knocked on her door for weeks.'

'Right, he'll turn up - let's go get Mitch. Kev, come on! KEV!'

'Coming!' Just wiping!'

'Bloody hell.'

'What's he wiping with, that's my concern!'

Cookie's eyes had flittered slightly at the sound of Kev's name being shouted somewhere nearby or far away. His head throbbed and at first he could only sense blinding light and a high-pitched noise. A tingling sensation ran up the length of his index finger and into the bone of his wrist. Forcing reluctant eyes to reopen despite the piercing glare, Cookie was able to take in more of his surroundings as he acclimatised to the alien ability to see.

First, he squinted at the almost-closed blinds that were still allowing far too much sunlight into the room - from the angle of which he was able to ascertain that time had passed since he was with the lads and getting annoyed, but not a great deal. The sun was definitely lower, but it wasn't yet after half eight; he could tell. It would have been duskier.

Guarded on both sides, the blinds were flanked by a mess of flowers and colours that at first seemed living, before becoming curtains. Ignoring the pounding in his head, Cookie turned and saw frame after frame of blurred photographs, in no conceivable order or pattern, covering the wall opposite him. For anyone with OCD, he thought, this would be hell. He smiled a little at this first rational and humorous thought, and immediately regretted the alteration in his facial muscles. Above the pictures, a narrow shelf ran the perimeter of the room about half a foot from the ceiling, adorned with ghastly, colourful ornaments of all different shapes and sizes. He had to assume this ran the entire perimeter, as he could still only see the wall in front and those on each side - he was not prepared to try to look behind or up just yet out of fear that his brain would implode.

The high-pitched noise seemed to have become a type of music he didn't recognise, but he wasn't sure when this had happened. When he was smiling maybe? When looking at the shelf? He simply couldn't be sure at all of when each sense was returning fully to him.

As the shadows and light from the blinds moved slightly, Cookie became aware of the warm feeling on his face and closed his eyes again. Sat opposite him, more a shape than a figure, Foz told him to worry. Or did he say *not* to worry. Cookie had missed the first word, obviously. Then, as the light burned his eyelids and his insides warmed to a glow, Foz was emptying desk drawers in an old, long-forgotten classroom, and replacing the contents with sand and muck. Cookie could feel his younger and current selves merging together and laughing, until the noise of his own mirth snapped open his eyes again.

The light shining fully on his face, he now saw himself reflected in the pictures opposite. Seeing his own face, and knowing there was nothing wrong with his head, sent a wave of relief over him. It hurt, but it wasn't bleeding or broken or battered. He felt his body relax slightly, apart from the buzzing agony in his right hand. The pictures now were clearer as the cobwebs of sleep blew away, and Cookie could make out that most, if not all, were group shots. Not your two to five people group shots, but at least thirty people in each photograph. Lined up. Posed.

Only one picture was different; directly in front of where he sat and stared at his own reflection, two pictures to the right, an almost ethereal image of a lady stared straight ahead out of the frame. Her face was expressionless, her eyes dark and her hair a white mane. She seemed to be glowing. She seemed also to have a group of people within her shining features, as though this were some sort of double exposure.

A cloud must have passed over the sun, because the light pushing through the blinds dropped for a moment, and in this split second, the photo became only another group shot. No lady.

As the light threw itself back into the room, and the beautiful warmth again caressed Cookie's face, the image reappeared.

This time, the lady was looking to her left.

Cookie, through the scathing pain of movement in his brain, turned to his right.

Chapter 13: Four Doors

'Where's the big twat gone, then?'

'He must have doubled back on us and gone to see how Bucky is getting on!'

'Bucky's fucked!'

'I think Mitch is the one getting fucked!'

'Been a while since we've heard from him! Someone message in the group?'

'I can't, me phone's not been working!', replied Gaz.

'I can vouch for that from when I was driving around looking for a shop that doesn't exist!'

'Sorry, mate!'

'What shall I say?'

'Erm…say something like we know you're up to your nuts in guts but it's lads night and we're coming to get you!'

'Concise!'

'Lads...lads - I've got a great idea!'

'Are you sure you don't need a piss mate?'

'That's where I had the idea! Well, when it turned to a shit! Well, actually, when I was wiping!'

'Kev, whatever this idea is mate, I don't like where it's going!'

'It's not that bad; do you all remember some of the things we would do with extreme rules nicky nocky?'

'Like what Bucky used to do?'

'Yeah, and I remember some others that I think Kev is alluding to…'

'Yes! So, Foz would always put a milk bottle on a door handle, knock and run and we just hear the glass shattering as we fled around the corner!'

'That was a fucking awful thing, looking back on it!'

'Yeah, there could have been pets or little kids stepping on rogue glass the next day. We aren't doing that, Kev!'

'Absolutely not - mainly because people don't get milk deliveries anymore - but I see your reasoning as well!'

'So what else, if no bottles or dick punches?'

'Well, Lee used to…'

'I used to do the 'shitstomp'!'

'Absolute classic!'

'We came up with lame names for things, didn't we.'

'Aw can we do that though, as adults?'

'Course we can!'

'We always targeted someone with a dog, because they probably deserved it at some point, so we just need to look out for the signs.'

'You going full Bucky on us? Rain Man of pranking?'

'No - I literally mean *signs*; Beware of the Dog signs are all we need to look for.'

'But where will we get the ingredients?'

'Ingredients? We aren't making a fucking cake!'

'What would you say?'

'I don't know...components? I suppose ingredients will do.'

'Good. Where will we…'

'Already sorted!' Kev pulled out the pick n' mix bag Hughesy had passed to him in the cemetery, bulging with something horrendous.

'Okay, let's do it!' responded Lee - my signature trick, so I'm going for it!'

'Good lad!'

'For fuck's sake!'

'Let's get looking then!'

'One sec…' said Dave, running up a side street and then reappearing seconds later.

'What happened there?'

'Knocked on, didn't I!'

'What about rule one? We all do one house!'

'Yeah, same house as last time!'

'Ooh, loopholes!'

'What rules are you talk…' asked Gaz, before being interrupted.

'Here's one! Beware of the Pug - little fucking rat things! Right, who's got a lighter?'

'No mate.'

'Haven't smoked since school!'

'Sorry, dude.'

'Mitch will have one! He's just around the corner!'

'Right, but this is the place! Knacker, do you mind nipping 'round to get Mitch's lighter?'

'No bother - it'll be worth it!'

Fat Knacker ran until he was just out of sight, and then slowed to a walk, breathing heavily. As he opened the gate and walked up to Marie's door, he noticed that the curtains were still slightly separated where she had looked out at Mitch tapping earlier. Glancing in, he caught sight of Mitch and Marie lying intertwined, but still mostly clothed, on the settee. Experiencing a conflict for about a second before the desire to see Lee's shitstomp for the first time since the mid-nineties won out, Knacker banged on the door.

The curtains moved, and he looked to see Marie, startled. She recognised him and gave a little wave. Then, Mitch opened the door.

'Mate, what the fuck? I said I'd catch up!'

'Yeah, erm, sorry. We would like you to be with the lads, you know, for this occasion, but right this second we need your lighter!'

'Here', Mitch rummaged around for an age, getting visibly angrier with Fat Knacker. 'I'll message later but I'll be quite a while - we're just chatting about old times, yeah!'

'Yeah, sure.'

Mitch closed the door, Marie waved again, and then she closed the curtains fully. Fat Knacker walked slowly back to where he would be seen, then ran around the corner back to the lads.

'Nice one; no Mitch?'

'He said he'll be ages!'

'Right, if I set this up, will you light it Hughesy?'

'Of course, it would be an honour and a privilege to assist in such a historic moment!'

Kev handed the once-white paper bag to Lee, who had to hold in a wretching response to the package; in the time since he had first shown it to the lads, the contents had started to seep through the thin paper designed for ten tiny sweets. Fat Knacker handed Hughesy the lighter, and together they moved through the gate, emblazoned with its 'Beware of the Pug' sign.

Stooping so as not to be spotted, the two made their way silently to the doorstep. There, Lee set the paper bag down on the centre of the slab of stone, and went to knock on the door. As he did this, his eye caught sight of a drop of something brown on his trousers. He instantly and automatically wet his thumb and wiped at it, as he had done with grass and blood earlier in the evening.

While Lee did this, Hughesy set fire to the disgusting device and pressed the bell. He then turned and darted silently toward the gate, glancing back to see why Lee had not moved.

Not hearing a knock, and content that his trousers were again acceptably clean, Lee stood up fully and put a foot up onto the step to lean forward and knock on the door. As he did this, the already-alerted occupants of the house (a man in his late fifties, accompanied by his wife of the same age) came curiously to the door.

Lee went to knock just as the door opened in front of him, and lost his balance, stumbling forward. Seeing a ball of fire on his property, the man instantly reacted by pushing his wife backward and stamping down on the flames in his tartan slippers.

Being stood essentially astride the package during the most exciting part of any shitstomp attack, Lee's chinos were splattered with faeces; heavily covered from the turn-ups to the knee, and slightly less so from the knee to the mid-thigh, with only a few smaller but obvious clumps between the mid-thigh and the waistband.

Hughesy burst into laughter, turned back to find the gate had swung shut and flipped forward over it at waist height, clattering to the ground. Still roaring, he gathered himself up and began to run.

'What the hell happened?'

It took Hughesy quite some time to gather enough breath to answer Kev. 'Oh, lads, I can't...'

'Where's Lee?'

'He's...he's...'

'Have we lost a fourth band member? We're shitter than Sugababes, us!'

'He's coming, I think, but wait until you see...'

'Hughesy, you fucking cunt - why did you press the bell?' asked Lee as he appeared around the corner, throwing a very brown cloth into a wheelie bin.

'Mate...I thought you wanted me to?'

'I just asked you to light the bag! Look at this!'

As Lee got closer, the rest of the group began to react to the image facing them. Horror quickly became hilarity.

'Will you all shut up!'

'What did you do?'

'Bloke came out and stamped didn't he! Thanks to this flid!'

'Honestly, I'm sorry...but this is amazing!'

'We really liked those chinos, as well!'

'Now you can all fuck off! Hold my phone, will you - don't want it stinking!'

'Has he called the police?'

'No. I said I'd seen this twat lighting the bag and ran up to put it out, just as he was running away. Old fella saw him laughing his tits off so believed that straight away!'

'What the hell - you blamed me!'

'Taking some blame is the least you owe me after this; I'm fucking covered in dog shit now!'

'Dog shit?' asked Kev.

'Yeah it's everywhere - fella gave me a cloth to wipe down but it's no use is it.'

'You think that's dog shit though?'

'Yeah, we always used dog shit - that's why we picked dog owners…what are you getting at?'

'Oh Kev', said Hughesy through gasping breaths, 'please tell me you're about to make this vision even better!'

'Kev, is this fucking dog shit I'm caked in?'

'No.'

'Big cat shit?'

'No.'

'Kevin…is this…your shit?'

'Yes.'

Hughesy began guffawing uncontrollably as Lee ran back and vomited into the same wheelie bin.

Chapter 14: Five Doors

'Mitch has messaged asking where we are; said he's on his way.'

'Thought you said he'd be ages, Knacker?'

'That's what he said - and how it looked through the window, if you know what I mean?'

'May as well walk back that way then. Tell him to stay put.'

'Will do.'

The light was beginning to fade, and the breeze was picking up slightly, as they rounded the garages and saw Mitch standing under a tree, as far out of sight of Marie's house as he could be.

'Hey, we've missed you, man!'

'Sorry lads, priorities got messed up but I'm here now and I'm going nowhere. Where's Cookie and Dave?'

'Dave?'

'He keeps disappearing and reappearing. Cookie, on the other giant hand, just up and vanished about an hour ago!'

'How can you lose a fucking juggernaut?'

'That's what we said. We went up the cem and then knocked on doors (without running) to try and find him, but he's pissed off home I reckon!'

'What a bellend. Can't believe you've been all the way up the cem!'

'Aw naw, it's just back there ten minutes, didn't take long!'

'Dave, lad - where've you been?'

'Knocking and legging it. I'm enjoying this!'

'Rule one was…'

'Yeah, we've said! He keeps doing the same house.'

'Clever.'

'Isn't it!', beamed Dave.

'And Gaz, nice to see you're awake.'

'Oh yeah, not been sleeping mate.'

'So what's the plan?'

'We were gonna head back here for you, then check in on Bucky!'

'Let's do that. On the way, someone please explain to me what happened to Gary Shitter's pants, and why we're still in his gang!'

With only Cookie and Bucky absent, the almost full group walked and talked, crossing in and out of alleys between houses as though they'd always lived there. Returning to the street where they had left Bucky, the sight in front of them was much different.

'He was right', stated Fat Knacker as they passed the house with the Passat and pink curtains; outside, watching the events unfold, stood a man and his wife in their thirties, and two girls looked down from the upstairs window.

Glancing between the fire engine and ambulance, the lads were able to ascertain that Bucky might still be some time.

Continuing their walk they crossed the small wooden bridge, the wheelbarrow not an issue for anyone any longer, being relieved of several beverages and a Gaz. They walked together around the opposite side of the boating lake to where the boathouse once had stood, and passed the hill where they had met a few hours earlier on their right hand side. Crossing the small metal bridge that separated the boating lake from the narrow pond, they walked up behind the VG and into a housing estate.

Meandering through still-familiar streets, Hughesy was the first to return to the game. 'Well, lads, I guess there's a few of us still to play.'

'Erm...you, Knacker, Gaz and Kev, I think. That right?

'Think so. I'm going now before it's completely dark - hard enough to see already. What's the time?'

'Nine.'

'Right. Rule two is in force.'

Hughesy stepped into a garden surrounded on each side by high trees, so the light was even worse. He walked swiftly to the door, knocked and began to jog back down the path. As his eyes grew accustomed to the darkness, and just before he left the garden, he knelt down and looked at something that had grabbed his attention on the ground.

Behind him, a light enveloped the garden as the door was opened, and a familiar voice, changed slightly by pain and age, said, 'Can I help you?'

Further along the path, Dave and Kev had walked ahead of the others, discussing the contents of Kev's bag and that Kev was preparing to unveil the nineties wonders inside. Toward the back of the group, Fat Knacker had hovered a moment next to a car underneath a streetlight, examining the swollen left side of his face.

'So what's in there, then?'

'You'll see soon enough!'

'Right, man of mystery…'

'It will be worth it - something to make everyone laugh.'

'We're having a few of those, it's good - past few weeks I've wondered if I'll laugh again.'

'Yeah, same…it sounds silly, but I think there are few heartbreaks as profound as the loss of a friend - a proper friend - who you grew up with and would have done anything for.'

'Totally agree. When I lost my Mam a few years back it ripped me up, you know, and then with Foz I've felt guilty that that's completely shattered me - like it's affected me more than my own Mam!'

'Don't feel guilty, mate. I get it.'

'And I think I know why, being with you lot here, why that is; it's to do with time.'

Kev waited for Dave to go on.

'She had her time. She was in her seventies and it wasn't expected, but at that age you're able to say those old cliches 'she had a good life' and that. But when someone your age goes, and is gone forever, before they even hit forty, what can you say, nothing, 'he lived half a life', it's bullshit, it's unfair, it's just not how things are meant to happen, or should happen, or do happen when you envisage adulthood as a kid, you get that?'

Kev nodded.

'Sorry mate. I agree, I guess I'm saying, that it's such a profound loss because we can't match it up with a reality we've always known. We know we will lose parents, grandparents...we never knew we were going to lose Foz so suddenly.'

'Mate, I love you! Take a bench, I'll be back in a minute and I will cheer you right up!

'It's Hughesy, Mrs Forrester. I came to...to pay my respects.'

'Oh, I haven't seen you for so long! Come in - Morris would love to see you as well!'

'Erm...okay, yeah - one second!'

Hughesy stuck his head out of between the trees and foliage, and just making out their shadows along the street, quickly told Fat Knacker he would catch up.

'Come on, son.'

'Sorry, I was just looking at the reef we - the lads - got.'

'Oh yes - they were all too lovely to leave at the crematorium so we brought them back until we can scatter the ashes somewhere!'

Hughesy followed Mrs Forrester into the house, stepping around the decaying flower arrangements and back onto the path. Inside, he followed Foz's elderly mother along the passage, past the stairs on the left where they'd tried to sledge down like Kevin in Home Alone, not realising the stairs turned at the bottom. He passed the kitchen on the right, where four years later they had made their first batch of brownies for the lads. He couldn't be certain, but the wallpaper looked the same, and the air hung in the hallway with the same scent of damp and Glade plug-ins. It was like being transported back in time.

'Morris must have popped upstairs - have a seat - it is lovely to see you! Cuppa?'

'Erm..just a water please, I've had a few drinks actually.'

'Nothing changes then!'

'It feels like lots have - but not now I'm here.'

'You're lucky you caught us up - we tend to go to bed by nine these days but Morris hasn't been sleeping so we've tried staying up a little later. I'll be back with that drink!'

Sitting alone in the living room, which had been decorated at some point since he'd last been here, Hughesy sank back in the armchair and realised how exhausted he was from pushing Gaz all over the place. When he closed his eyes for a moment, his ears pricked at the familiar, hoarse voice of one of his best ever friends.

Sat opposite him, roughly the age they last spent every day together, rather than the last few times they'd caught up over the years, was a teenage Foz. Blonde-tipped curtained hair hung around his face, and the silver chain on his neck looked like it could leash a tiger. His eyes were bright and always moving, just as they always had been, and his mouth turned up into a smile at one side. Foz raised his hands, palms upward, as if to say 'what the hell are we doing here', and he rolled his eyes.

Hughesy smiled, and reached forward with his fist outstretched, ready to bump. Foz lowered his hands, and said 'I miss him', just as Mrs Forrester reappeared through the doorway to the passage.

'Here we go, dug out some Wagon Wheels as well - you would eat a pack together in one sitting you two!'

She sat in the spot that Foz had moments ago occupied.

'Thanks, just the water. Not much has changed at all in here!'

'Well, you're the one wearing the same coat you had in school!'

'Fair point, Mrs Forrester! Fair point, indeed!'

'So, you wanted to pay your respects, you said?'

'Yeah, there was a mix up and we didn't get into the crem…the crematorium, sorry.'

'We just saw Gary in there out of all you lads!'

'Gareth, yeah. Sorry about what happened after the service!'

'What's that? Are you with the others now?'

'That's right, yeah. So we've all got together tonight for a drink in his memory, you know!'

'It was a lovely service, really lovely!'

'Good; what songs did he want playing?'

'Oh, he'd never considered that sort of thing! We played that one, by the brothers…Morris will know it. Morris!'

'We really wanted to be there - we've been telling stories tonight, and thinking about the old times.'

'I bet there were a lot to tell!'

'Too many.'

'He missed you, you know. All of you. He hated the silly pranks and things you all got into when you were teenagers; he was glad when you all matured.'

'Oh…'

'We saw David quite often, with his partner, they'd come around or go for a drink. He still lives just across the boating lake there!'

'He's with us tonight!'

'Lovely man, considering!'

'Consider…'

'Morris! Come down! The Hughes boy is here. I'll have to go get him, he never answers me - deaf you know!'

'Okay, but I'll have to get off soon, I've disturbed you enough.'

'Nonsense. He'll be home soon anyway!'

As Hughesy was left alone, perplexed by the last comment, he started to wander around the room, looking at the cards on the mantelpiece and the little keepsakes that people had brought around. Picking up the cards Hughesy glanced at a number of 'sorry for your loss's' and 'we're here for you's' before realising they were all to 'Helen'. Just Helen. In one he read the line 'at least now they can look after one another' and then his eyes rested on the dusty, patterned urn in the centre of the fireplace.

'I don't know where he's got to!'

'What - sorry?'

'Morris, he isn't answering me.'

'Is that…unusual?'

'Well, I suppose it's more frequent these days, with his hearing going - we are old now you know!'

'Perhaps he's finally getting that sleep you said he needed?' replied Hughesy, hoping not to upset Mrs Forrester. 'I'm going to go now, but I'm glad I got to come and see you.'

'Me too. Will you do me something? Will you take this…' Mrs Forrester handed Hughesy a small, plain silver can. '…and scatter him somewhere that would have meant something to him? We tried and couldn't think of anywhere special enough.'

'I couldn't…'

Mrs Forrester thrust Foz's ashes into his hand, before embracing him as though it were her last time ever holding her own son. Without another word between them, they walked to the front door, and Hughesy walked down the path.

'Would you look at all this mess!'

'What, Mrs Forrester?' said Hughesy, looking back.

'Someone has dumped all these old plants in my garden!'

Sitting no higher than his shoulder and staring up into his eyes, was an old lady. She was expressionless, with dark eyes and a white mane around her head. She was dressed entirely in black with her dress buttoned up the front right to her chin. Her face glowed much the same as its reflection, with the light from the blinds covering her whereas it only stuck to Cookie in strips of light and dark.

'What the…'

She slapped him. The speed at which she moved made liars of his senses which had suggested she were elderly.

'Don't swear, young man.'

'I…haven't heard anyone get called that since school. Where the fu…' She slapped him again.

'Where am I?'

'You are in my house.'

'Why?'

'You came onto my property, did you not?'

'I don't know…'

'You did. Had you knocked rather than pressed the bell, like your little friend, you would have walked away again.'

'What friend?'

'Gary.'

'Who the f…who's Gary? What's going on?'

'Don't play dumb, young man.'

'I wish I was…do you mean Gaz? I thought he was called Gareth!'

'There are some things we are going to put right.'

'Okay.'

'First of all, you came onto my property, intimidating a poor, defenceless old lady. Secondly, you have always been a bully. Thirdly, you are going to learn what it feels like to be helpless.'

'Look, you've lost me, pet! We were playing a silly game that's all…call the police if you feel intimidated. It certainly doesn't feel that way just now.'

'I can deal with your sort more effectively myself. Don't go anywhere.'

The lady stood from the seat on Cookie's right, reached beside the settee and pulled forward her walking frame. She then steadied herself and began to push herself slowly toward the door on Cookie's left. Closing it behind her, Cookie was left alone in the room. To confirm this was true, Cookie forced his excruciating head to turn in every direction and make sure there were no creepy old men on his other side.

'My sort?'

The echoing of his own whispered voice made Cookie shudder.

'You're canny fucked' said Foz, sitting now on a stool near the window, mostly in shadow.

'Can't swear here - Rose West will knack ya!'

The silhouette vibrated as though laughing quietly, then asked 'do you not know who she is?' as though Cookie should.

While trying to find an answer to this question, Cookie realised Foz was gone again, and that he did have some inkling as to who his captor was.

'Captor? Fuck that!'

Trying to stand, Cookie became aware that the pain in his head and shooting up his wrist were nothing compared to the feeling of absolute nothingness in his legs. No sensation whatsoever. It wasn't as though he couldn't get to his feet, but once there the total numbness between his toes and his mid-calves meant he collapsed backwards into the settee. On the third attempt, he threw himself forward with such velocity and ferocity that he did not fall back, but rather carried forward into the wall with the photographs on, smashing his face into one of the group shots and sliding to the floor. Despite the massive noise caused by the commotion, the old lady did not reappear. He closed his eyes.

Chapter 16: Gravel

'Well, that was a nightmare!'

'Where were you?'

'Only went in Foz's house, didn't I!'

'His Ma's house!'

'Yeah, Dave, you know what I mean.'

'Sorry, I was up ahead and didn't notice where you'd gone. Knacker just said you'd catch up!'

'I was coming out the garden and there's our bloody reef, so I stopped and ended up going in.'

'Knew I recognised the street.'

'I recognised the whole house inside, mate. Don't know what made me knock on there - it's as though I was drawn to it.'

'She's not what she used to be, mate.'

'What's up with her, like? Foz's Ma and Da were always having the lads 'round - they were class!'

'Aye, but his Da died a few years back…' said Dave.

'That's the nightmare part! I completely forgot about that at first - I wasn't here for Foz through all of that - and she's acting like the old man is alive and well!'

'Fuck off!'

'Proper Norma Bates?'

'No, man - she just doesn't know!'

'Wow.'

'Then as I'm leaving, she's completely forgotten Foz has died as well - she doesn't know why there's flowers in her garden! Poor sod.'

'She doesn't know if it's Monday or Norway?'

'Not the time for that!'

'Blessing, maybe?'

'What? How the fuck can that be a good thing? Always looking for people who aren't there?'

'I'd rather be looking and be disappointed than be left all alone in the world with nobody I loved around. For her, I guess they're always at the shop or in the shed.'

'She thought Morris was upstairs', added Hughesy, pulling out the Aftershock bottle and seeing it off.

'Morris?'

'Foz's Da!'

'These people have names?'

'Ma's called Helen!'

'Bloody hell...have all of your parents got names, then? This is mindblowing!'

'Haha...it was a sad thing to see, that's all.'

'Maybe a blessing?'

'Alright, we don't need to go through that again. Where's Kev? Piss? Shit? Pissing shit? Shitting piss?'

'Hobo said he had a surprise for us. Finally showing us what's been in that bag he got out of the car!'

'Yeah, he rushed back there - said he'd be a minute but that was ten minutes ago.'

'I'm coming now lads! Prepare yourselves!'

'If he comes near my chinos with a dripping bag of his own fucking brown bile, I swear I will kick his bastard lips off!'

'Waheeeeeeeeeey!'

In the relative darkness of the park where the group now sat, all huddled closely on one bench apart from Lee who had been made to sit on the next bench along the path, about ten yards away, they all heard Kev before anyone saw him.

Like a low-budget superhero, from the descending darkness, wearing massive orange foam headphones attached to a clip-on Walkman, Kev came hurtling past them on his all-too-familiar bright blue rollerblades with fluorescent yellow wheels.

'Did anyone else just see what I saw?'

'If it was California Kev, product of nineties Saturday morning TV, then yes.'

'Waheeeeeeeeeey! I've got rollerblades, ladsssssss!'

'We can see this. You're fucking thirty-nine pal!'

'Don't be ageist!'

'I'm not...will you come back into view? I'm being realist - you're probably going to kill yourself and then we'll have to carve 'being a bellend' on your gravestone!'

'Howay, I'm canny impressed he can still ride them!'

'Is it called riding? When it's skates?'

'Well, pilot them sounds a bit too advanced.'

'Semantics!'

'Suckmadicks!'

'We really haven't grown up at all, have we!'

Kev zipped past again, singing 'she only cums when she's on top' from *Laid* as it played through his headphones.

'What makes you say that?'

'Haha - so Gaz, Kev and Knacker, just you three left?'

'Well, we don't think Cookie bothered despite the goon's big speech. Message him and see if he's coming back!'

'What speech?', asked Mitch.

'He went off on one, had a go at everyone, stormed off saying nobody would mess with him if he banged on their door so he wasn't running, then he bloody ran away like a bitch!'

'Really? Where was this?'

'Few roads past where we left you - thought you were going to be ages, actually!'

'That is what you told me!'

'It is mate, I'll fill you in later. Right now, I don't see Cookie doing a runner if you ask me - he's always the first one in and last one out of the party!'

'Messaged him just now in the group: Where are you ya fucking roidhead gayboy?!'

'You trying to piss him off further?'

'He won't know who said it - it's in the group chat, man!'

'Are you serious? Look above your comment…'

'…it says Lee!'

'What? Why? Dave, when did you get my phone?'

'You all knew I wasn't on social media - I can't send my own messages to the chat, can I!'

'You better tell him that was you! I'm putting up with enough shit for one night!'

'Now it's dark, you can't really tell - it looks like it's a pattern or something!'

'Aye…crapoflage!'

'That's when you handed me your phone by the way, just before you hurled.'

'Where's our resident Bodyform advert gone?'

'No idea. Gone to a rollerdisco, perhaps?'

'I am genuinely impressed with him on those things...I think I'd struggle to ride a bike.'

'Think the bike would struggle to have you ride it, Knacker!'

'I'm just large set - can't do anything about it. It's not fat!'

'What is it then? Cake and gravy?'

'Piss off.'

'You know it's only banter, right? Love you really, dude.'

'Banter or batter!'

'I know, yeah. Just taking some getting used to when nobody's called me anything negative for twenty years.'

'Really? Your woman not seen your dick?'

'To be honest, I've not seen it since 1992!'

'Haha...what is your name, Knacker?'

'My name is on Facebook, and apart from Dave you're all on there!'

'I remember it from Primary, actually.'

'Wait...that's your real name?'

'I thought that was a joke!'

'Yeah - thought it was just a pretend name?'

'No, why?'

'Well, it sounds fake. And stupid!'

'Mate, Knacker *is* actually a better name.'

'You reckon?'

'Abso-fucking-lutely!'

'Better than when you all used to say 'Knacky', I guess.'

'Come on then, Mitch. Why were you so quick when Knacker clearly thought you'd be hours?'

'Really? We aren't going to forget about this?'

'No chance.'

'Well, obviously I saw Marie and tapped on the window 'cos she was right there, and went in. She'd been decorating and had the furniture all covered up, except the settee was pushed right into the centre of the room.'

'This is the exact opposite of a Gaz story!'

'It's all relevant, lads. So she cracks open a bottle of wine and we're stuck chatting like a foot from each other on this one two-seater. We were just chatting about old times, and Foz fucking up her social life and our relationship. We got to talking about marriage and she's divorced - told her I'd recently split with my Mrs (dunno if I'd told all of you lot)...'

'We'd seen the car porn and kind of guessed.'

'Pornhubcaps!'

'...very good - so then her hand is on my knee and we're laughing, you know, then we kissed then we were getting quite fucking frisky...'

'Get in, lad!'

'...until that cunt turns up! Marie saw him first, looking through the window like a sex pest - a proper Lee! We jump up just as the tool brays on the front door. Marie goes to the window 'cos her jeans are half undone, and I go to the door. This prick wants my lighter, which is in my pocket but I've got so hard inside my jeans that my cock is up and to the side, and the lighter is trapped. This arsehole just stares at me.

'I thought you were just begrudgingly giving it up!'

'Where is it, actually? Cheers, Hughesy! Anyway, he goes, I get back inside and we explode onto the settee. I mean it's lusty as fuck lads, pants straight down and we're at it before he's wobbled out the gate!'

'But within minutes you had left!'

'Been a while, had it?'

'Not because of that! Because her three startled little kids were suddenly standing there! Watching my hairy arse pounding mammy!'

'Fuck, no way!'

'Brilliant! Absolute classic!'

'Had you not seen she had kids?'

'Did you not pissing listen? She was decorating, man! I pulled out and dove over the back of the settee, landed on a fucking trike, face-to-face with shitloads of covered picture frames that would have given the game away had they been on the walls in the first place, and yanked my jeans up.'

'This is amazing. As if you weren't going to tell us this!'

'I'm not done.'

'There's more?'

'Oh please, let there be more...'

The group paused for a moment to watch an ambulance pass to their right along the main road at the top of the park. Lee had moved closer to listen to the story, and on the blue flashing illumination of his faecal trousers, was sent back to his bench.

'So in that time, Marie's dressed and sat consoling her bairns, telling them everything's okay and I'm there to help with the decorating.'

'Bet you were!'

'Planning on emulsioning the walls!'

'What does that even mean?'

'Sorry, lads - I was trying to be rude.'

'It's about to get ruder! Thanks to this bellend banging on the door instead of tapping on the window, those kids have been startled awake and are worried. Marie is calming them down and trying to usher them back upstairs, when the little lad (he's maybe five) points and laughs!'

'At what?'

'Fucking hell - obviously I'm fully erect while we're shagging, so I've been trying to get a trike out of me arse, looking at photos stacked on the floor and quickly pulling me jeans up at the same time...'

'Oh I like where this is going!'

'...and I've trapped me cock, pointing directly up to my belly button, with the waistband of my jeans. I've tightened my belt, not really thinking because by then I was standing up pretending to be a fucking painter and decorator, and this kid is now pointing at my bellend, fully purple and restrained, peeking out of my jeans like that Kilroy or whatever it was called that we used to draw on subway walls!'

The gradual building of stifled laughter overflowed, and they all burst into those proper, uproarious belly laughs that you don't experience enough once you've stopped hanging around with your teenage friends. Their faces were contorted into various expressions of delight, horror and sympathy all at the same time, tears streaming down their cheeks as the blue flashing lights came around the bottom of the park and pulled up outside a garden just a hundred metres away.

'Where's Kev?'

Chapter 17: Six Doors

'James there with their...Nakatomi and Children of the Night...' declared Dr. Fox as the tape cut off the end of one song and jumped to the start of the next. Kev realised he actually missed the awful homemade tapes recorded from the radio, with snippets of DJ mutterings where you couldn't press record and play at the right time.

'I'm gonna do mine now, lads!' said Kev, as he passed them again, noticing Dave messaging someone as his phone vibrated in his pocket. He had mastered the rollerblades incredibly well, he thought; much better than he expected to when he'd put them in the car at his parents' house just before five o'clock.

Behind their current seating arrangements, across about a hundred metres of grass and obscured slightly by trees, was a long row of houses that weren't the most expensive in the area, but certainly had some of the nicest views across the park.

Because of this, they had low hedges or fences and Kev could see as he sped towards them that most of the properties were occupied and still lit up for this time on a Saturday night. Opting not to wake anyone, Kev made the instant decision to go for the illuminated house directly at the end of the pathway across the grass. This meant he would be able to zoom straight in, knock, turn, and get his speed up again very quickly, disappearing back into the dark of the park.

As he got closer, and thanks to a nearby streetlight, he was able to see that the garden was clear, with no fountains or washing lines or discarded kids' toys, and there were no steps to the door. Perfect.

'Fight for the future of our nation' resounded around his head as he left the pathway and entered the open gate.

'Let's come together and unite...' as he was catapulted through the air.

'Nothing's gonna stop us now', rather ironically, as the glass door stopped him dead.

Hearing a sudden crash as he turned the telly off and stood to head up to bed, the owner of the house could not fully understand what he was seeing at first.

Looking out from his living room, and along the corridor to the front of the house, he could see his front door, or what was left of it. Hanging haphazardly, tangled in the frame, was a scruffily bearded man of about forty, wearing those popper bottoms that he hadn't seen since he was a teenager. One leg was completely undone, and bleeding. The head of the man was pointing toward the floor, while his midriff was caught on the middle separating beam of the frame, and his legs were dangling outside. The door was half open, despite being locked hours earlier, suggesting a significant impact. The glass in the top half of the door was shattered all over the passage flooring, which also was now home to a Walkman, the old cassette-playing sort, which appeared to be emitting some sort of rave music. This unusual time-traveller was made all the more confusing when the man noticed the blue rollerblades, with still-spinning fluorescent yellow wheels.

It was a couple of minutes before Kev came to - face to face with a man more concerned than angry, but certainly still bubbling with vitriol. The position he was in was incredibly uncomfortable and meant that the man was crouched on the floor to look him in the eye.

'Don't move!'

'I…sorry, man!'

'What happened? What are you doing?'

'I'm erm…I was rollerblading!' replied Kev, realising how stupid that sounded out loud.

'I can see that!'

'I…'

'Did you come down that path from the park?'

'Yeah.'

'I think you've just gone too fast and then come straight through the gate!'

'I should have stopped? I can stop?'

'I think you've hit the gravel, pal!'

'The gravel?'

Kev looked underneath himself, through the intact window, between his own dangling legs and at the upside-down garden. Unseen from the path as Kev approached, the entire garden was that red and pink gravel that people put down when they're trying to look posher than they actually are. Along the length of the garden, instead of a pathway to the door, were five or six small, hexagonal paving stones, spaced about half a metre apart.

Kev then remembered the feeling as he passed the garden gate, his rollerblade hit the unexpected surface and he sailed through the air. In what must have taken less than two seconds, he watched his own ridiculous appearance, lit up by the streetlight, collide with its reflection.

'Fucking hell...I'll pay for this!'

'I'm worried you already are, mate. Try to stay still - the ambulance is on its way.'

'Thank you. I don't feel bad - just uncomfortable!'

'I would still stay put until they arrive...we don't know what's under you, you know, the glass is smashed everywhere and you're obscuring the worst part of it.'

'I will. Can you do something with my head though - I feel dizzy!.

The man returned to his living room, and promptly came back with a footstool. Carefully, he slid this under Kev's head while easing his top half up very slowly, constantly confirming that Kev felt okay. With his head resting on the footstool, Kev began to calm. Quite clearly, he suddenly heard all of the lads burst into hysterical laughter, probably in the same place he'd left them, and he wondered what Dave's message had said.

'Here's the ambulance now!'

'Thank you so much - I will pay you for the damages!'

'Accidents happen don't they? Just tell me something?'

'Sure.'

'Where the hell did you get Adidas poppers?'

The vibration in his pocket woke him. Face flat against the carpet, shattered photograph just next to his head, Cookie was aware that the light was now completely gone. He reached around with his right hand, but the pain in his finger and wrist was now much worse. Instead he had to use his left hand to get his phone out of his right hand pocket, which, with no feeling in his legs, was more difficult than anything else he had ever done. Eventually he was able to get the phone, after almost giving up with his left hand crushed under his twenty-two stone, twisted backwards into the opposite pocket. He was thankful at least that he was wearing this stupid Kappa tracksuit, which had some give, rather than the jeans he would have normally opted for. In doing so, and because of the angles and pain, he had not noticed the hip flask slide out of the shiny red nylon abomination.

Reading 'where are you ya fucking roidhead gayboy?!', Cookie's anger raised a notch. When he got the use of his legs, worked out what the fuck was going on and got out of this place, Lee was going to get it. The energy it had taken to get the phone wasn't totally wasted, as he managed to send 'wherver uleff me' with his left hand before the door opened.

This time the old lady wasn't using her frame, but pushing a little silver tea trolley and using that to support her weight. As she trundled into the room, she noticed Cookie against the skirting board and the little trail of blood on the wall. He had just finished pushing his phone into his left hand pocket and was lying totally still.

'Oh dear.'

She came closer, leaving the supports of the trolley and using the wall instead to steady herself as she bent down to pick up the photograph. As soon as she touched the oak frame in front of his forehead, Cookie was ready to grab her by the arm and demand explanations. He waited as she got closer; he could hear her wheezing breath as it got louder and then, when he thought she was right above him, he opened his eyes and shot out his left hand.

Nothing. His eyes fell over the picture in the absence of a body, and he saw the old lady, much younger, among the group in the photograph. He knew her, but didn't know from where. Perhaps, he thought, she was someone's Nana from school.

His phone vibrated, then he heard her wheeze again and realised she was bent over his bottom half. Slowly pushing herself back up the wall to a standing position, he managed to roll his top half over without being sure if his legs had done the same or stayed facing the floor, like a broken He-Man figure.

In the hand that was not holding onto the wall, and more alarming than anything he had considered thus far, was a needle. She looked down at him, smiled without changing her expression, and said 'young man, we are going to talk'.

Chapter 19: Door Six

'I hope this isn't anything to do with Kev!'

'I feel it will be. He's probably shit himself to death in someone's shed!'

Crossing the grass rather than walking around the path that Kev had taken, the group were at the edge of the garden at the same time as the paramedics were kneeling down to survey the bizarre scene.

Across a gravelled garden, with stepping stones leading to the door, the Paramedics were knelt just outside. The door itself was slightly ajar, and a pair of legs stuck out from about midway up the frame. These legs were very familiar, clothed in antique sportswear and finished off with the blue and yellow rollerblades of yesteryear.

'For fuck's sake', whispered Lee.

'This is shit!'

'No, *this* is shit', replied Lee, pointing at his chinos. *'That* is appallingly bad!'

'Shhh…listen.'

Straining to hear, the group were able to gather quite quickly that Kev wasn't badly hurt, that the man on the other side of the door seemed quite relaxed and understanding about everything, and that the paramedics were going to move Kev.

'I'm so sorry, this must be the stupidest thing you've seen in a while!' said Kev.

'Actually', responded the lead paramedic, 'it's been an unusual night.'

'This might be the second stupidest, believe it or not', added the other.

They moved Kev together, with the man on the inside guiding his head and shoulders. As they steadied him on his feet, from which the rollerblades had been removed, Kev felt around his stomach area and legs. Relief washed over him as he realised he was okay. There were a few cuts, and would definitely be some bruising, but the poppers popped back together and that was the main thing.

The rest of the lads had moved slightly out of view, when Bucky appeared from the opposite direction. Under the streetlights it was clear to see that the colour-changing t-shirt had definitely been a mistake, as the sweat patches were enormous, particularly on his left side.

'Lads, lads, lads!'

'Bucky! About time!'

'I know, I know! I've been messaging you lot, then I saw these familiar lights and thought I'd take a punt!'

'Have you?'

The lads, apart from Dave, Fat Knacker and Gaz, looked to their phones where they had a number of messages in the chat.

'Sorry mate, we've been howling.'

'See. Been looking for you lot for the last twenty minutes! I saw Cookie wasn't with you either so I had a look for him.'

'He went home.'

'Not what he says in that group!'

'Oh shit - Cookie's back where we left him apparently!'

'Eh? We checked that whole street!'

'How long's he been missing?'

'Since about half seven!'

'That's well over two hours. Where the hell could he be?'

'Shit…'

'Speaking of…those chinos have become a lot more desirable!'

'All this going on and everyone's still bothered about my fashion choices!'

'Fashion's pushing it.'

'Have you seen the state Kev's got himself in?'

'No, where?' Bucky looked around the group and saw Kev leaving the garden.

'Are you with *him*?' asked the paramedic.

'Erm…oh yeah, he's back. I am, yeah!', replied Kev.

'That makes a *lot* of sense', responded the second paramedic, as Bucky waved to them.

Rejoining the group, his Reebok t-shirt and poppers dotted with specks of blood around the area that had been stuck in the doorframe, Kev embraced Bucky as if he hadn't seen him since they were teenagers, rather than a couple of hours.
'How you feeling?'

'Very sore, think my arm's going to be a bit bruised tomorrow! You?'

'Very bruised, think my everything's going to be a lot sore tomorrow.'

'Here's your bag!'

'Let's finish off tonight first though, eh lads - before we start thinking about real life tomorrow.'

'Have you kept the game going?'

'Oh yes - just Knacker and Gaz left!'

'Young man'. He couldn't place it, but someone had called him that in that same way a long time ago; as if 'young man' meant 'little bastard'.

His phone had vibrated a few more times, but was now silent again. He had been instructed to push himself up onto the settee again - he was used to tricep dips - and was back in his original position. His legs were still there, but that was only confirmed by sight.

The old lady looked wilder now; her dark eyes were invisible in the twilight and her white mane caught all of the light in the room. She stood leaning against the tea trolley, holding a crutch in her right hand. The crutch was resting across the trolley, so she did not have to take the weight of it, but could (and did) jab Cookie with it every time he moved forward slightly.

'Young man...'

There it was again. His head was coming out of all fuzziness now, and he felt like he could almost clutch at the memory of those words.

'...you need to learn to treat people better. You are, and always have been, a nasty little piece of work.'

'I don't know you, or what it is you want or have done to me, but I'm sorry. Whatever you think I did to you, I don't know what it is.'

'Not just you - that whole little gang!'

'What gang?'

'You, Forrester, Hughes, Buck, Lee, poor impressionable Gary, that fat boy...'

'Knacker?'

'...the gay one, that Kevin boy *and* Mitchell!'

'Who are you?'

'Just someone else who's been at the brunt of your horrible antics.'

'Well, we're not like that anymore. We're all mature, responsible...businessmen, parents...'

'Except Forrester! He died. I read that in the paper!'

'Yeah, unfortunately...'

'Un? Un? One less bully in the world!'

'Look, I'm getting pretty pissed off...' She jabbed Cookie with the crutch. '...and slagging off...'

She jabbed him again.

'...that's not even a fucking swear...'

She jabbed at him and he grabbed the crutch in his left hand. Pulling violently, she bounced off the side of the trolley and fell out of his view. Cookie grabbed the trolley and started to pull himself to his feet, falling slightly. He pulled, as he collapsed backward, the tea towel covering what he assumed were biscuits on a plate, and fell back to the settee in shock.

Moving the tea towel fully, he saw the syringe she had held earlier, and a number of glass jars. Cortisone. He knew what that was; his Grandad had used it to numb the pain from arthritis in his last few months. But here, and dated in the last week, were three empty bottles. Three. In a week. She can't have used that many unless she had...

Cookie stopped.

He tried to lift one leg, then the other. He had no idea what the potential effects of this massive overdose could be, but was instantly glad that he wasn't a tiny little twat like Kev or someone. Also, it was a relief to know what was happening to him; it seemed to make him feel like he could control it. He concentrated all of his energy and mind, clouding out the tiny voice telling him to turn the bottles over.

Gripping both sides of the tea trolley, he dragged himself to his feet. Another vibration in his pocket and he pulled out the phone, glad it was on his left side. A few messages from Bucky since he last messaged the lads himself, which actually made him feel better that he knew he was okay, followed by one from Lee.

He knew he had to get outside. Deciding on dragging, rather than lifting, his feet, Cookie unsteadily started moving toward the front door, which he assumed was to the right of the now darkened window; a sliver of streetlight only just managed to creep between the blinds where the sunlight had streamed in earlier. In this minimal light, only the shocking white of the old lady's hair stood out in the middle of the room - face down and motionless.

It seemed to take an age to reach the inner door in the back right corner of the room, which was perhaps only five feet from where she had first been sat next to him on the settee. Opening the door was impossible while holding onto the trolley - if the trolley was there, the door would open only far enough to bounce off it and close again. Cookie therefore had to abandon his supports and lean against the wall adjacent to the window. Finally opening the door, he slid through and found himself in a cupboard - large, expansive, but without exit.

'Fucking hell...', he flinched as he said it, expecting the lady to pop up and smack him in the mouth again. He pulled out the phone, and replied to Lee's message. He hoped they knew where he was, because he really was running out of ideas. He remembered, still clearly, shouting at the lads and nothing further. The instant appearance of an ellipsis underneath his message sent hope surging through him. It was late now, but the lads were still around somewhere. While waiting, he turned the phone around so that the light from the phone illuminated the cupboard.

'Get in!'

Chapter 21: Door One

Looking back toward the group, Bucky removed his watch and glanced at the time. It was only just after seven so plenty of time to have everyone act like idiots for a bit, then just enjoy being together. On arrival at the VG earlier, as he'd received a text from Dave asking for alcopops, he'd felt an overwhelming urge to be the instigator, as though that was his role in the absence of Foz. He had there and then decided to buy as much old school booze as he could find on the shelves, and actually felt like he was getting away with something when they served him. He had asked Mitch to accompany him with the wheelbarrow later on because he knew, from his miserable life taking photos of his car, that he'd be up for anything. Having two of them lay out their plan was much more convincing. Group mentality, or something. A little voice had nagged at him to shut up as he spoke to the others about the tribute, but he'd ignored it and been excited by their excitement until this moment. Now, he thought it was possible that the voice may have had a point, *but* the lads were watching.

He gave a thumbs up and then reached up to press the doorbell. Lifting the flap again, he positioned his hand just inside the letterbox, fingertips against the inner flap (he thought of a great rude joke to tell the lads later) and watched as the rectangle of light on the front of the door lit up. The emergence of a shadowy figure through the distorted glass built his anticipation, and he felt a surge of excitement overpower the tiny sprinkling of doubt. He knew he'd not thought this through properly, but wasn't quite sure what he had missed.

Bucky had never been the one to back down, back out, give up or give in - no matter how stupid his actions inevitably were.

Just as the handle began to move, and knowing he should stop and make up some excuse about checking the structural integrity of local doorsteps or something, Bucky thrust his hand forward into the house.

Inside his house moments earlier, Dicky was just about to eat a frozen lasagne and watch the rest of series 3. He had about six episodes to go, but no plans for Sunday. On his fold-out table, he had arranged his plate, cutlery, the remote control and a can of Morretti. Then, his doorbell rang.

Rolling his eyes and moving the little table to one side, he headed for the front door. Automatically, despite the blazing sunshine outside, he turned on the hallway light as he entered it. It occurred to him he always did that, no matter the time of day, when answering the door. Through the window in the front door, he could see the shape of his truck and the blurred outline of the houses opposite, but this view should have been interrupted by whoever was calling around.

'Fucking kids', muttered Dicky as he reached the door and started to open it. Almost as soon as he had begun moving the handle downward, he noticed a shadowy figure below the window, and then a hand shot through the letterbox.

Despite the fact that he had stepped closer than he normally would to look down at the shadow, the fingertips of the hand stopped mere millimetres from his crotch. The arm was tattooed, and was about half a forearm into his house. The fact that this wasn't a kid made Dicky's attitude change completely, from simple pissed-offness to sudden rage.

He pulled the handle the rest of the way down and swung the door open as violently as he could, ready to push this unusual intruder back off his step (avoiding the freshly waxed truck, of course) and giving him the hiding he deserved.

Instead of this logical cycle of events, when he thrust the door open, the body attached to the arm was dragged screaming into his hallway. Dicky did his best to leap out of the way of the flailing limbs, and found himself on his own step, staring at the back of whatever moron was now stuck in his door. His mind leaped back to the cooling lasagne and he kicked the figure in the side out of pure frustration and confusion.

'What the fuck, fuck off, man!', screamed Bucky.

'Me fuck off? I'll fucking kill you!'

'It's not what it looks like!'

Dicky looked at his own door, with its new addition. Was it wearing a Hypercolour t-shirt?

'What is it then? 'Cos I'll tell you now, it looks like some cunt has just tried to punch me in the cock through my letterbox, and I've not known that shit go on for fucking years!'

Still facing the door, and unable to see the man behind him, Bucky closed his eyes and tried to come up with something. He felt like his shoulder had been dislocated by the force of the opening door, but it was the sharp pain in his forearm, where it was trapped, that really worried him. His arms were bigger. That was what he'd not considered. He had been showing off to the lads, explaining his infallible system for working out who to prank, and not actually considered that he wasn't the same eight stone teenage boy that he'd been.

'I've come from the council...to check the erm...structural integrity of doorsteps!'

'You what?'

'Yeah...erm...so we had a lady fell because of a wobbly step last week...we're testing them all in the area for safety, you know!'

'That doesn't explain why you're stuck in my fucking letterbox!'

'Oh...so I was checking the step, and a...bee flew into your letterbox, so I put my hand in to stop it getting into the house...and I rang the bell to warn you, but then it stung me!'

'I'm ringing the police.'

Bucky slumped as much as he could, as the man stepped over him and strode into the house and out of sight.

'Bucky...what the fuck - are you okay?'

'Kev, I'm stuck.'

'No, come here...', replied Kev as he pulled Bucky backward, causing the sharp pain to increase ten-fold.

'Get off, man! He's ringing the police! You lot just go.'

Dicky returned along the hallway, asking 'What are you doing there?' to the second figure crouched behind the first.

'We can't just leave you, dude!'

'You have to...I came up with the rules didn't I! I didn't expect it to be me after just quarter of an hour. I really thought we'd lose Knacker!'

'Right. We'll be back. Message when you can!'

As Kev ran away, Dicky enquired 'Fat Knacker?'

'What?'

'Did you just mention Knacker?'

'You know the fat fuck?'

It was at this point that Dicky bent down facing Bucky, from inside the house. 'You horrible little bastard, Bucky!'

'Dicky...you're fucking kidding! What the fuck did you boot me for?'

'Why are you trying to grab my goods?'

'It's a long story!'

'When I said I hadn't known this shit for years, I didn't expect you to be an actual ghost from the past, you prick! Why are you dressed like you've just finished a shift in the Broom Cupboard?'

'It's a really long story, mate.'

'Well, I think we have some time, seeing as you're stuck to my door!'

'Do you have any ideas?'

'I'll ask Jarmain next door, he's good at the handyman stuff and I've just fixed his car.'

'Passat?'

'Yeah, his wife chose it - sick bitch!'

Having knocked on for Jarmain, Dicky returned and went into the house; he arrived back at the door with a lasagne, three cans of Morretti and a curious look on his face.

'I'm going to eat my tea, you're going to tell me this long story.'

Dicky unfolded a deck chair and sat down to eat. He handed a can to Bucky, who couldn't open it one-handed and gave it back. Jarmain appeared, was given the third can, and spent five minutes laughing unhelpfully before his wife came around the side of the garage and told him he shouldn't be drinking at this time on a Saturday.

Having been of no assistance at all, except suggesting they remove the door from the frame (but Bucky would have still been clamped in place), he left again as the police car arrived, sirens blaring and lights flashing.

Much like Jarmain, the two officers offered very little but laughter. As Bucky relayed the story of the night, what had happened to Foz, the fight outside the VG (which the police had attended on request of the Happy Shopper staff, but found no culprits in the vicinity), they called for an ambulance and a fire engine. Bucky tried to protest, but Dicky explained his arm was looking very purple by this stage, and the officers explained he would need to be cut out of the door by the fire brigade.

For the first time since hearing the word 'Knacker', Dicky felt angry again. Sure, it was a silly prank, but if it was going to cost him a whole front door, Bucky better pay up.

'This isn't great like, mate.'

'I am sorry!'

'I know, but what if this had been some random's place? This could have gone much worse for you!'

'He's right', interjected one of the officers, 'you'd be charged with assault, criminal damage maybe, unlawful entry! I hope these mates of yours have seen sense and aren't carrying on your daft idea!'

'I'm sure they will have.'

'And how many of you are there?'

'There's ten...no, nine sorry, without Foz!'

'You do know you can't meet in groups of more than 6 outdoors!'

'There's six, yeah. I said nine because I was...erm...thinking upside down.'

'Right, well I strongly advise you do not all meet back up, and if we spot the others they will be warned and possibly fined as well.'

'Really? Is there not real crime to focus on?'

'Nothing really ever happens around here. You've been warned!'

The officer turned and walked down the drive, got in the car and started the engine.

'What would you have been doing tonight?'

'I was going to watch...Peaky Blinders, pal, until you showed up.'

'It's nice to have a catch-up though, right?'

'I guess so - better under other circumstances!'

Bucky, aching at every joint from the unusual position he was having to adopt to alleviate pressure on his shoulder, heard the departure of the police and arrival of the ambulance and fire engine behind him. These were followed by lots more laughter and unhelpful comments.

The plan was to use cutting equipment to slice the door in half horizontally, from the hinges to the left hand side of the letterbox, and from the locking mechanism to the right hand side. Moments before this was attempted, and much to the relief of Bucky *and* Dicky, Jarmain reappeared and suggested they unscrew the letterbox at both sides, as sliding that off over Bucky's hand inside the house, should allow him just to remove his arm with the outside half still attached, leaving the door intact.

The firemen and paramedics praised him for a moment, before his wife told him to get back in the house so the girls, who were watching from their bedroom window, didn't think he was involved in this awful behaviour.

As two firemen moved Bucky backwards and helped him to his feet, which were alive with pins and needles, his joints creaked. One of the firemen visibly recoiled when he saw the ridiculously huge purple neon patch of sweat under the trapped arm. At this moment, with the whole estate out watching the events unfold, Bucky heard the screeching of the wheelbarrow wheel, followed closely by the lads roaring with laughter.

Looking towards the sound, Dicky shouted 'alright lads!'

'Hey, Dicky! How's it going?'

'Uneventful!'

'Bucky, catch up ya prick!

'Yeah, yeah - I'm trying!'

'We're heading back over toward the Park!'

The creaking wheel and laughter faded, as the two paramedics began working together with a fireman and his boltcutters to break the letterbox away safely from Bucky's arm. Having done so, the firemen left the scene, once more confirming that Dicky didn't want the police back to press any charges.

'We just need to make sure there's no longer term damage to the tissue or muscle here - you have been trapped in that position for a couple of hours.'

'Okay, but I would like to go soon as - I can pop into the walk-in centre tomorrow if there's anything still wrong.'

'Oh, there's going to be a lot of bruising for a while, I would think.'

'Yeah, just seek more attention if it seems worse or the colour starts spreading to your lower arm.'

'It's already losing some of that purple hue, mate, to be fair!'

'Cheers for your medical input, Dicky.'

'Here, I reckon I'm entitled to any input I want, don't you?'

'Sorry....'

'Why is Knacker dressed as Slimer?'

'Hadn't thought of that, he is isn't he!'

'Maybe it's the closest he'll ever get to *slimmer*.'

'Sorry, again...I am! I'll drop some cash around tomorrow, or Thursday when I sober up!'

'You better! Do me a favour mate...'

'Anything.'

'Never come to my door again!'

At that, Dicky folded his chair, closed his door with the rectangular hole where the letterbox had been two hours earlier, and returned to his seat to watch the rest of Desperate Housewives.

Chapter 22: Seven Doors

'I'll let Cookie know we're coming looking for him', said Lee.

'He'll probably smell *you* coming!'

'I still can't believe you let Kev shit in a bag and you took it to a door.'

'I didn't fucking know it was his shit, did I? Cunt let me think it was dogshit!'

'I never actually said it was dogshit...'

'To be fair to Lee, you didn't say 'this is a handy parcel of my own excrement' did you!'

'Well, no...'

'Prick!'

'At least you don't look like a paedo anymore - no self-respecting kiddyfiddler would cake themselves in shite to attract the young'uns!'

'We gonna find Cookie then go up the cem to see the night out?'

'Been, Bucky.'

'All the way up there?'

'Did none of us ever realise it was directly above the estate we knocked about in? Why did we walk miles around in a circle?'

'What else would we have done? It's not like there were people to do or things to see.'

'You mean things to do and people to see?'

'No, I don't.'

'Speak for yourself!'

'I think the less you say about Marie, the better!'

'What's happened with Marie?'

'You missed a lot, pal!'

'I've literally missed all of the fun tonight, even the fight!'

'Wish *I'd* missed that!'

'Still sore, Knacker?'

'Yeah. I'll live.'

'You don't even know Knacker's real name!'

'Ah well, I don't wanna know that! Always a Fat Knacker to me!'

As the group passed over the metal bridge and the hill on their left where they'd started the night, their phones began to ping one after the other.

'It's Cookie again - he's being weird.'

'It says 'hurry up crazy lady can't walk in cupboard'.'

'What lady can't walk in a cupboard? Why is she walking in a cupboard? He's fucking mortalled!'

'I've replied saying we're coming back now to find him!'

'Chuck a can out of there', Fat Knacker said to Hughesy as they neared the wooden bridge. 'I'm definitely not driving home!'

'Need some liquid courage as well? Just you and Gaz to go.'

'Yeah, we'll see.'

Instead of walking into the estate this time, Bucky veered left off the bridge and followed the path of the beck as it ran around the edge of the houses.

'Avoiding Dicky's?' 'Something like that.'

'Well, this way we avoid Marie's as well, so I'm game for a detour.'

'Me too - I've left shit all over a doorstep and sick all over a bin - I'll not be going near them again!'

'Well, I'll catch you over the other side', said Dave, as he ran into the estate and out of sight.

'What's his deal?'

'He's been torturing some poor twat all night - keeps hitting the same house to get around your first rule!'

'Clever Dave!'

They walked in a half moon around the estate, meeting up with a giggling Dave at the tip of the crescent. Following the path ahead, they soon arrived at the end of the gated private street, and filled Mitch and Bucky in on the last time they set eyes on Cookie.

'Well, he must have gone into one of these houses, mustn't he!'

'Yeah, but we knocked on every house.'

'Nothing unusual?'

'Not really - Lee recognised someone's nana from back in the day, mostly elderly or families with kids.'

'Yeah but she wasn't a Nana - I can't think where I knew her from but it wasn't from knocking on for people.'

'Well, let's start over.'

'It's after ten - we'll be waking people up!'

'Start with the houses with lights on then.'

So they did. Disgruntled and sleepy residents, one after the other, explained that they hadn't seen a giant dressed like Vicky Pollard this evening. Three houses remained in darkness.

'I'll try this one', said Knacker. In the back of his mind he was deducing, because the curtains were open and the house was in complete darkness, that nobody was home. The plan was, therefore, to count this as his Nicky Nocky. It wouldn't be his fault that nobody was put out or angered by his presence.

'I saw Cookie walk a lot further down the path than this though, Knacker.'

'Can't rule it out!'

'Okay, we'll start heading along.'

Fat Knacker was very fat. This should already be clear. He was also incredibly unfit, and lazy. For this reason, he did not even bother to speed up his walk, confident as he was that he was approaching an empty home. He reached the bottom of three steps before he heard the low, menacing growl.

To his despair, this noise did not come from the other side of the uPVC door in front of him, but from half a garden behind. He turned, telling himself not to. A huge, black dog, snarling and edging closer as if ready to attack, stood next to a shed that had been mostly obscured by the late hour's darkness. The only bright thing in the garden, coincidentally, was Knacker himself; a massive, bright green, dog toy. He took a step backward, knowing that he had nowhere to go and couldn't outrun any breed of dog, let alone this one. His heel met concrete, and he lifted it backwards onto the first step.

The dog suddenly broke its stationary state, as if a motor had revved and was now set free, and hurtled towards Knacker at breakneck speed. He tried to step up again, tangled his treetrunk legs and fell against the white door. The sheer weight against the light plastic frame forced it open, Knacker fell backwards into the house, and just as the beast reached the door frame, its chain choked tight and yanked it back into the garden.

Knacker stared in disbelief, as he saw Hughesy's shocked face appear at the open garden gate to see what Knacker was doing. The snarl became deafening as the dog turned and sprinted at Hughesy, who realised what was going on just in time to close the gate. Looking through the patterned lattice in the six-foot wooden doorway, Hughesy stared straight at Knacker.

He stared back, and began to consider his options before the dog realised, with what looked like delight around its foaming mouth, that the force of running at full speed in one direction and then the other had loosened the stake holding its chain from the ground. It fixed eyes on Knacker and turned away from Hughesy, emitted another, louder snarl and broke into a gallop. Fat Knacker managed to lift his right leg, and slammed the door with it while still lying on his back.

The door had not broken, but rather just given under the weight, and the lock clicked as it shut. A second or less later, the force of the dog collided with the door, but this time it held.

With the second crutch tucked under his armpit, Cookie felt infinitely steadier on his feet as he read Lee's reply.

They were coming to find him. But if he didn't know where he was, how would they? He had to make his way to the front door of the house; had he even knocked on this door? Maybe he had, but why had he come in? It still didn't quite add up, and who the fuck was this woman who kept calling him 'young man' and knew all of his friends?

He picked up a torch - he hadn't tried the lights, but why not? Something had made him not even consider pressing the little white switch on the wall, but that was the most logical thing to do. The rest of the shelves were crammed with books and more photos in albums, each with a date: 1974-1975, 1983-1984, 1991-1992. The most recent one he could make out was 1994-1995, and they started sometime in the early 1960s. Who dates things between years - a football manager?

There was definitely no exit but the one Cookie had entered through, though it was clear that a doorway had been bricked up at some point. He turned, steadied himself on the crutch and started to move back into the main room. He faltered a second and replied again to the group chat. Still fuzzy, he tried to just give the facts and replaced his phone in the usual pocket.

Shuffling back into the living room, the darkness was all-encompassing. He again ignored the light switch, but this time felt a pang of fear as though he were going to be badly hurt if he pressed it. Irrational, he thought. Then, correcting himself, he decided that given recent events, anything was rational. The darkness was almost blinding, and just as he went to press the button on the torch, he realised why.

Somewhere he heard a dog barking manically, as he realised that the one source of light when he'd entered the cupboard, the crazy mane of white hair, was not in the centre of the floor.

He then realised he had not had to circumnavigate the trolley that he'd left no more than a foot in front of the door. Pushing the button on the torch with his right index finger, the burst of pain and fire in his hand and wrist sent him flying backwards over the steps and into the long grass again. That was not an irrational fear, he realised, but completely justified given the electric jolt he had been given hours earlier. He now knew what had happened outside.

'Fucking bitch', he said loudly, as he turned on the torch. At the same time as the circle of light scanned the room, Cookie asked himself a question that should have occurred to him long before now. He simultaneously heard a banging sound emanating from the room ahead of him, to the left of the settee where he had first awoken. The sphere of light answered that new, obvious question as soon as he had it firmly in his mind.

Chapter 24: Door Seven

Panicking in the dark, Fat Knacker rushed into the front room and to the open- curtained window. Hughesy was still at the gate, gesturing for him to go around the back of the house. Feeling his way, but mainly guided by the streetlights which illuminated most of the rooms very well, he started to navigate towards the back door.

The house was definitely empty tonight, and a note on the kitchen bench confirmed that a neighbour was coming around each morning to walk and feed Cujo out the front. Fat Knacker was relieved, and even more so when he saw there was a key in the back door. Looking out of the window at the rear of the property, it was instantly clear that he wasn't going to be able to leave through a back gate, as there was none; also, large conifers lined the boundary at the rear. His only option, other than going back around the side of the house and trying to outrun the dog, would be to climb onto the barbecue against the right hand fence, and jump into the next garden.

Fat Knacker had always despised garden-hopping. When they'd decided not to do that tonight he knew he was the most relieved. However, he also knew he had no choice and that there were at least seven gardens before he came out on the far end next to the old cem again. He'd hated that place even more.

Knowing physically this was possibly going to kill him, he unlocked the door from the kitchen as silently as he could. He was still acutely aware that the dog could probably get down the side of the house, although there may have been a gate.

More tentatively than he had ever done anything in his life, he stepped out onto the back step. Without thinking, he let the door swing shut behind him. Panic overtook everything and he bolted for the barbecue, leaped onto it and was halfway over before the dog appeared and leaped, snarling at the fence.

Landing in the next garden, Fat Knacker saw that although the lights were on, all of the curtains were drawn. He jogged across the lawn and used a child's slide to step up and over the next fence. The child would probably be upset by their concave slide the next day. Similarly, in the next garden, a handily-placed water butt next to a stone plant pot made for a climbing apparatus, and he was into the fourth garden.

Fat Knacker was feeling extremely good, halfway down the row of houses already, when he straightened up from his landing position in the fourth garden.

Chapter 25: Names

'Knacker's in trouble!'

'We've made a right pig's ear of this get together haven't we!'

'What's happened to him? Diabetes?'

"The Hound of the Knackervilles has got him - he's ended up inside the first house on the corner. Doesn't look like anyone's home though. I gestured to him to stay put so he'll just wait there until we go back for him. Sure we can distract a dog between us once we've got Cookie.'

'Right - poor sod missing out again!'

'He's just a proper soft cunt isn't he? Reckon he was always late back in the day just to avoid exercise and trouble.'

'Worked for him; he's the most successful out of all of us - and have you seen his bird?'

'Haha has *she* seen *him* though?'

'Must be doing something right!'

'Aye - he's a wet clit! Does what he's told, never going to risk anything or do anything dangerous!'

'He's a cappuccino!'

'You've made that shit joke before.'

'Right, this is just the house where the little old lady lived', said Lee.

'Okay, let's have a knock on.'

'You don't wanna disturb her, man!'

'Why?'

'She's little and harmless - probably be terrified by us coming to the door!'

'We'll just take a sec!'

'Perhaps you shouldn't go now that you look pebbledashed!'

Bucky and Hughesy walked up through the garden, which was overgrown with dying plants and weeds. It was Bucky who stepped up to the door, and went to ring the bell.

'I knocked on earlier mate - think she was canny deaf 'cos I had to bang a bit!', shouted Lee from the gate.

'Cheers!' Bucky knocked, loudly, on the door.

After a few moments, an old lady appeared. Her face was expressionless, her eyes dark and her hair a wild, wiry tangle of white. On her forehead, a welt was forming and a small trickle of blood weaved amongst her few wrinkles.

'Are you okay, love?'

'What do you want?'

'Sorry to bother you. We're just looking for a friend of ours - Cookie - really big lad!'

'Looks like Hellboy doing a sports day!'

'Ignore him, love. Have you seen him?'

'I saw Gary out there earlier and spoke to Lee and told him I hadn't seen Cookie.'

'Okay, are you sure you're alright?', asked Bucky, just as they heard a thud from somewhere in the house behind her.

'Just a little fall, it happens. My son is inside, he'll fix it up. I'm fine. Goodbye.'

'Sorry to bother you.'

They heard the key turn in the lock and the distant snarling anger of the dog again as they turned to step back down to the garden. This latter noise was closely followed by a clattering of metal.

'Something's been moved there', said Hughesy, nodding towards a large depression in the centre of the grass on their left. 'Canny big.'

'Could have mowed the rest', muttered Bucky.

Leaving the garden, Bucky stopped and looked at Lee for a long time.

'What, have I got a television on me head?'

'I know her.'

'I said that.'

'Hughesy, did you recognise her?'

'Familiar, yeah...'

'Can't place her face though, can you?, asked Lee.

'Right let's try the last one.'

'Wait, Lee...did you tell her your name? And that his was *Gary*?'

'Why would he? His name's Gareth.'

'My name's Gary!'

'Is it mate? And no - why?'
'She knew your names.'

It had never happened that Cookie had looked up at someone. He had never known how it felt to be everyone else. In fact, for a period in his twenties he'd thought it very humorous to tell people in large groups that he'd been all of their heights, but not one of them had ever been his. He'd never been this guy's height.

The thought that had struck him moments earlier, as he balanced on one crutch and panned the beam of light across the empty floor and over the gallery of group shots, was that after he had been electrocuted, he had awoken on the settee. This tiny woman, with her unusual filing system (that stopped in ninety-five, that was significant, but why) and her lightning hair, had not moved him. Four of her couldn't have. Who had?

Cookie had his answer. As this behemoth's hand crashed into his jaw, he wished he hadn't called her a 'fucking bitch' though. He deserved it; it was foul language after all. He dropped the torch while trying to hold onto the crutch with both hands and stay upright. As he hit the floor again, he heard the old woman talking to someone beyond the door.

There can't be more of them, he thought. The man stepped over him, and he tried to grab the trolley to pull himself back up but it toppled over. Managing to get to his knees again, Cookie swung and connected with the midriff of his opponent, who felt it, but not as much as he had hoped. The pain in his fist was far worse, but he swung again, just as a foot collided with the underneath of his jaw and sent him backwards.

The muffled talking stopped suddenly, and the door sounded like it was being closed. Cookie felt for the phone in his left pocket, but it wasn't there. The torch cast a halo of light on one side of the room, and as he rolled over Cookie saw the man reaching down for him. On the floor, to his right, was the syringe which had fallen from the trolley along with the other contents. He grabbed it with his right hand, using all of his will to clench that fist around the object. As the man grabbed him by the collar of his bright red tracksuit top, Cookie repeatedly hammerfisted the side of his face with the syringe.

Screaming, the man rose up and staggered back toward the window that had let in so much light hours earlier. Through his open mouth, Cookie could see the syringe where he had forced it through his cheek, which was now pinning his tongue to the other side of his mouth. The door behind him opened, and synthetic strip-lighting cast a yellow glow across the scene, as the old lady wrapped around his back.

'You've always been a vile young man!', she screamed, repeatedly hitting him in the head with the keys in her hand.

Cookie spotted and clawed for his hip flask just under the settee. He stood up, for the first time feeling his legs doing as they were told, and propelled forwards into the howling hulk in front of him. Cookie thrust his shoulder into his groin, and lifted upward, sending the man backwards through the window, clinging onto Cookie's head in a headlock, the old lady still hanging onto his back.

As the three of them fell earthward, a shattering hail of glass erupting around them, Cookie saw Foz standing to his left, by the fence. He smiled, the moonlight catching his blonde-tipped curtains, and said 'it's *my* fault'.

Chapter 27: Fences

Fat Knacker was feeling extremely good, halfway down the row of houses, when he straightened up in the fourth garden.

There was a slight stitch in his side, but the feeling of being a proper lad, even if there were no witnesses, overrode that. He didn't so much jog across this garden, but rather he sprinted - it was a feeling he hadn't known since primary school. He sprinted, grinning and leapt at the next fence just as he heard an ear-piercing scream, which made him hesitate slightly when he was in full beast mode, followed by the shattering of glass. He couldn't stop, but he didn't jump either.

Instead, Fat Knacker ran straight into, and through, the six foot fence. As the façade fell forwards away from him, he saw Cookie, in mid-air, looking directly at him. He was sandwiched between two of the most contradictory figures you could imagine. Underneath Cookie as he hit the ground, a foot or two in front of the top edge of the now felled fence, was something bigger than Cookie himself. This beast was screaming, its face contorted and disfigured but appeared it would have looked the same without the pain it now exuded. It relinquished its grip on Cookie's head on impact; although outweighing him, he still brought at least twenty stone down on the creature's stomach, knocking all air from it.

As it reeled, the bright red phantom in front of Fat Knacker began pounding it in the forehead with a rectangular silver object.

The noise of the dog made its way to Fat Knacker's ears once again, as it reacted to the screaming, the shattering of glass and breaking of fences. At the other end of the scale, a tiny, wild-eyed woman with a crazed tangle of bright hair had held onto Cookie's back. She looked toward Fat Knacker, and he looked back at Ms De'ath.

What the fuck was Cookie doing with Ms De'ath? Was he protecting her from this other monster?

She then turned her attention back to his friend, and he noticed the blood coming from his skull where she was repeatedly stabbing him. He wasn't protecting her, he was fighting both of them. Cookie then did something completely unexpected - he pushed up and away from the massive mountain of a man who posed the biggest threat, and reached up with his right hand, plucking Ms De'ath from his back like an insect. Fat Knacker could not move or speak, before Cookie brought her down at speed into the patio paving. He then stood astride her and brought his huge fists down repeatedly on her tiny, old face. She remained expressionless throughout.

Fat Knacker grabbed Cookie and pulled him backwards away from their old teacher, not expecting Cookie to turn on him as well.

'What the…where the hell did you come from?'

'Over there; you were just looking at me!'

'Foz was there…this old cunt has been going to…'

'Ms De'ath?'

'…torture me or…who? No, fuck off!'

'You remember what happened to her?'

'I do. Shit man, this *is* all Foz's fault!'

'She was always a crazy bitch!'

As fat Knacker steadied Cookie on his feet, which had very nearly returned to a state of full functionality, Ms De'ath's son rose from the ground, slowly pulling the needle from his face. They watched as he pulled it first from his tongue, which flopped back to the bottom of his open mouth, and then disappeared from inside his mouth altogether, pulled the skin of his cheek almost to a point, and then was free.

Some teachers were good at what they did, some were terrible. Some were friendly, some supportive and some disinterested and dismissive. Some were Ms De'ath.

'Every school has one!'

'Do you think? That bad?'

'Maybe not quite that bad, but pretty awful?'

'She's vile. She belittled Foz for saying 'winder' as in to wind something up, when it was meant to be phonetical. Really went in hard on him, calling him a 'thick young man' and a 'waste of space'. He protested, saying the rest of Oliver Twist wasn't written phonetically so why was this one piece of speech; she was having none of it.'

'What was it meant to say?'

'Window, but it was spelled 'w-i-n-d-e-r' 'cos Bill Sykes was speaking.'

'She looks for anything, doesn't she.'

'You know Foz though, he just smiled and nodded and then as soon as we left the classroom he tells us he's got a plan.'

'A plan?'

'Oh shit - what was it?'

'Wouldn't say - he said we'd find out this morning on the way in, but I waited ages at the VG and the dickhead never appeared.'

'Did you keep an eye over by the school railing? That's where he usually walks up!'

'Yeah I did. No sign.'

'My big brother's just got a mobile phone. That's what we need. It would stop us missing each other on a weekend as well!'

'You're the only dickhead who doesn't turn up, Knacky!'

'Well, what time this week?'

'Every Friday, five o'clock at the VG, mate. Every single Friday it's the same. If you're not there by half past, you've got some searching to do.'

'It's not like we go far! VG, boaty, cem, park. Take your pick!'

'I'm not walking all the way up the cem by myself, it's miles away.'

'You're just scared of the place!'

'Am I fuck.'

'One day you'll admit it!'

'Why would he be scared when there's nobody buried there yet?'

'I don't know - he always avoids coming up there.'

'Lads, lads, lads!'

'Where were you this morning; I waited at the VG!'

'Had to go a different way and nip into Boyes! They open early on a Wednesday!'

'What did you need in Boyes? Are you starting to sew? Collecting Tupperware?'

'Something like that!' Foz pulled out of his bag a silver flask.

'We drinking at school?'

'It's not for alcohol!'

'Then what? You going camping?'

'This, my 'young men' is a two-litre metallic silver flask, with built-in cup.'

'Amazing!'

'Startling discovery!'

'And it is the exact same one as...drum roll...Ms De'ath's!'

'Erm...I don't follow.'

'Me neither.'

'The old hag wants to treat people like shit, and wants to belittle and put down every kid she teaches, so she's going to experience some changes.'

'Such as?'

'In this flask is steaming hot, fresh tea. I made it in my flask then poured it across to this one outside Boyes.'

'Hate to break it to you, but she drinks coffee!'

'Durrrr, that's the point!'

'You can say 'durrr', but I 'aint following!'

'When do you follow anything, Gaz?'

'Harsh but true.'

'Do I need to spell this out?'

All of the lads nodded.

'Bloody hell - when we're all eighty I'll still be the one explaining everything!'

'I can't imagine you reaching forty, to be honest!'

'Brutes - okay, so Death drinks coffee every day, right! It stinks, doesn't it! She opens it up, peering at us with those creepy eyes, makes all that noise when she sips it - it's horrible. I am going to make her a flask of tea. Every. Single. Day.'

'Why would she drink it?'

'I'm going to swap them out when she's not looking!'

'Oh wow - this is brilliant.'

'I know. So every day I will walk to school with a flask of tea, and walk home with a flask of coffee.'

'So you bought two flasks?'

'Gaz, will you keep up with what he's saying, please?'

'I don't get it still.'

'Can you imagine, making coffee every day and every day you take a swig of tea.'

'This really is playing the long game, though!'

'Too rights! She's been there since the sixties or something, torturing kids!'

'Yeah my Da said he'd had her back in the day.'

'My Ma was the same - said she'd never been nice to anyone!'

'Except her boy went to our school, left a couple of years before we started. Apparently she was always much, much worse to him. My Uncle was telling me that she'd burned his face once punishing him for swearing in the house.'

'Fuck off!'

'I've heard that too - pressed it against the hob and slowly turned up the gas!'

'She's got to get it!'

'For generations of kids!'

'Past and future!'

'Hope this works, mate!'

'It will - and then we'll start level two!'

'There's a level two?'

'There's *always* a level two!'

That day, for the first time, Foz switched out the flasks. Only Dave, Fat Knacker and Kev were in the same English class, but between the four of them they relayed the events back to the others on the way home from school.

Ms De'ath had particular things she did during a lesson; one of the reasons students were distracted and bored was that she kept a strict routine and made no effort to engage learners with activities or personality. Her lessons followed a set format of register, lecture for twenty-five minutes, a five minute period where she had each row of desks approach her and display the notes made from the lecture, then twenty minutes of reading or writing. In silence, too, apart from this awful instrumental music she would play. All of this was in silence for students, unless answering your name or a question. You would not be asked a question if you were paying attention - these questions were not designed to support learning, but rather to embarrass and punish.

After speaking for so long, and then talking to students, which she clearly detested, Ms De'ath would take a drink. Throughout the lesson, the flask would stand untouched until those last twenty minutes when you would be subjected to whining music and slurping sounds.

The lecture section that day had been about Victorian society, and could have been very interesting delivered by any other teacher. Ms De'ath then asked the rows to come out in her usual order - left to right, front to back. Her desk was on the left of the classroom, and she liked to sit the students she had a particular hatred for at the front, next to her. She could then call them out first, and set them their writing or reading task before anyone else. The longer they wrote, the more mistakes she could look for; the more mistakes she found, the thicker they were made to feel.

Foz sat at the front left, so he was called forward first. It visibly annoyed her to see he had made all of the required notes, so she informed the class loudly that you would have to be lazy not to underline your date and title. She then sent him away while looking at the next book in the queue. Behind the line of classmates, Foz lingered until Fat Knacker was at her desk. He sat at the end of the left-hand row and when his shadow obscured her desk, she would call for the second row. So that she could watch him as well, but with a little less venom, she had Kev sat at the front here, so he was next in line behind Fat Knacker.

Foz reached behind Knacker and in front of Kev, as the former deliberately said something stupid and got her full attention and wrath. He switched the flasks, and returned to his desk, stuffing his new flask into his bag.

Once everyone had been up to the front, she demanded silence and heads down. Within a minute, although it felt like an age, through his blonde-tipped curtains dangling in front of his eyes, Foz saw her reach for the flask and exchanged a glance with Kev, who was also pretending to look down very badly. They didn't dare look to make sure Knacker and Dave were watching, for fear of breaking her thirst in favour of beration.

Ms De'ath unscrewed the silver lid that turned over to become a cup. She placed this on the desk, and unscrewed the inner lid, and placed this next to the cup. She continued scanning the classroom as she poured the 'coffee' into the cup. Still not looking at the drink, she picked up the cup and cradled some of its warmth in her hands, and then took a sip.

Her expressionless face and dark eyes gave away very little, but there was a pause in time where she sat perfectly still, with even her wild black hair motionless. She blinked, ran the tip of her tongue across her lips and looked first into the cup, and then into the flask. This second action - as though there might be coffee in the flask but somehow it turned into tea on impact with the cup - caused a noise from Dave that bordered somewhere between a strangled cry and a sneeze. Her eyes darted toward him, but everyone was working.

Then she turned her attention to Foz. Hair hanging down in front of his face, she stared for a long time unsure whether he was looking back at her or actually, finally, doing his work. Without looking away, she drank off the tea, replaced the inner lid, wiped the cup with a handkerchief and replaced that, and stood the flask back in its usual position.

'What? She drank it?' asked Cookie.

'Yeah, man. No reaction! It was a massive letdown...'

'It was perfect - exactly as I'd hoped!'

'Eh? How?'

'I don't want a reaction yet. I want a reaction sometime between May and the end of the school year!'

'You're bonkers!'

'Think about it - all these years and generations, she's been pranked before; I want to go big.'

'Can we not just put a water bucket on top of her door?'

'Don't be a spaz, Gaz.'

'What then?'

'You'll see.'

Over the next few weeks and then months, a number of things happened. Each was more subtle, and more meticulously planned.

After about four weeks of switching flasks, and being almost caught a number of times, Foz stepped up the game. He told the lads she was starting to crack, after he had seen her sat in the car park, sniffing her flask of tea. For over a week, Foz had swapped the containers but Ms De'ath had not unscrewed the lid or poured a cup or taken a sip. The flask stood, untouched at all times. The lads had suggested she was no longer bothered, while others had wondered why she kept putting the flask back there. Foz had confirmed the new flask he picked up each day was hot, so she was still making the coffee.

The answer was simple; she kept making the coffee and standing it in the same spot on her desk as she always had, because she always had. She was not going to be defeated by one of these little cretins, even if she didn't know which class was doing it. Being equally vile to all students at all times, meant she could not be sure who was targeting her. In her mind, she was being vile *because* they targeted her.

Seeing her check the flask, in her car, confirmed to Foz that the game was still very much afoot, and that it was time for level 2.

'You're going to what?'

'Clear the walls!'

The planning for this one had to go up a notch, and Foz spent a long time going through the phone book and ringing as many of his classmates as he could from his house phone. Explaining, and begging some of the nicer students, he convinced the majority of the class to take part in his next 'harmless bit of fun'. Some of them had become aware already of the flask-switching, and wanted in on the action anyway. Others, and because no matter how perfect a student they were, they were shouted at and embarrassed by Ms De'ath, would see this as their only chance to rebel.

The classroom was almost a perfect square, with Ms De'ath's desk at the front right, which she called the left because of the way she was facing, which always caught someone out. Along the left wall, from her perspective, ran windows that started about four feet from the ground and went up to the ceiling. These looked out onto a yard, from which Foz thought another passing teacher had spotted him with the flasks on day nine.

Every other wall was pasted with dull, wordy posters on every inch of space. These were all Blu-Tacked in place; you could tell because the tac had sweated through the corners of the paper, as it does with age. Behind her desk was a blackboard (the kind that rotated three different boards, but which she only ever used the forward- facing option so that if a student hadn't copied it down before she wiped it, she could tell them off) and then posters all the way to the back right hand corner (from her perspective).

Along the wall to her far right was a door in the closest corner, and then more posters. Foz had ascertained, somehow counting them without getting wrong, that there were forty-one posters in total.

On a Friday, she would see their class last lesson and at the bell, would gather her bag and flask and stand outside her classroom door, ignoring the goodbyes of the students and locking it after the last one had left. The worst offenders were always the first to leave, followed by what she referred to as the swotty ones.

As everyone left the room, Foz ran to the far right wall, directly along from the door, and laid flat on the floor behind the back desks. From here he could see the legs of his fellow students passing out, then the door swing shut and hear the key in the lock. He then stayed flat. He could not stand up until the windows were obscured, as other staff would be ushering kids towards the gates.

Having the involvement of the swotty ones was perfect; standing chatting to each other along the wall, in little groups and huddles, any teacher would see which students they were and assume they were going to an after-school club or revision session, and carry on straight past.

At the other side of the yard, next to the science block, Lee and Cookie were starting to push each other, playfully at first then more aggressively, quietly at first then louder. All teachers' eyes were on them, and not the nice kids next to the English rooms.

Being old Blu-Tac, simply pulling the posters firmly from the bottom removed them from the walls, bringing all remnants of where they had been stuck with them. Foz was relieved, as he'd expected to be pulling off Blu-Tac as well. It took him around two minutes to clear the room, survey the brightly lit empty walls as the afternoon sun blazed in, and let himself out of the classroom using the deadlock on the inside of the door. Years earlier a kid had been locked in a classroom, so they'd had to put in key locks that could be opened from inside without a key.

By the time Foz appeared Cookie had Lee by the throat, and the pair looked like they were really going to get into it. Hearing Foz tell them to leave it, they both stopped, smiled, apologised and walked away together, much to the confusion of the three teachers who had been trying to separate them.

The kids along the wall dispersed, and everyone went home for the weekend. That Friday and Saturday night Foz wasn't himself - desperately wishing the weekend away whereas he usually relished every second of it.

On Monday morning the sun wasn't facing the English classroom, so the walls were not empty at all; without the afternoon sunshine, they were sepia, with forty-one bright rectangular patches of different sizes covering three sides of the room. Ms De'ath did not acknowledge this in their presence, and they wished they had seen her walk into the room that morning, but it was brilliant nonetheless. It was better.

The whole class, not just the four of them, sniggered and giggled and smirked throughout the lecture and the instrumental writing.

They had all - the whole class - had a taste now, and this made things easier for Foz. He was still swapping the flask every day, but now he was replacing it with hot chocolate one day, Bovril the next, tea the next, fresh orange the next, water from the beck the next and so on. He was unaware how close he was to winning his game.

'Why bother?'

'She's pouring it out. Every day she pours something else out when she gets home.'

There had been a couple of standard pranks thrown in along the way to appease the lads, who didn't always follow the longevity of his vision and needed instant gratification. On one occasion Gaz had walked into the staff room and taken a set of keys, which they'd then used to replace all of her desk contents with sand and mud. The walk to school that morning had been laborious, all of them laden down with the weight of their prank, except Fat Knacker who apparently forgot about it. Cookie had stayed lookout, although he spent most of the time watching what they were doing and laughing. As they had walked away, Ms De'ath had spotted a group near her classroom as she returned to it, shouted after the 'young men', but they had carried on walking and disappeared into the corridors.

They had let Gaz fill a bucket with water one day, which he had promptly dropped all over himself on the way to school. He could not understand why they found it hilarious that he'd filled it at home in the first place.

The day that Foz won, and therefore all students won, was mid-June. The plan was relatively simple, but involved everyone in the class. This wasn't a problem, as they had all been part of the ongoing shenanigans since 'poster day', but Foz rang everyone again the night before to give very clear instructions - he couldn't have anybody breaking rank or getting too excited and energetic.

So, the next day, they sat in their bare-walled classroom, with the new filing cabinet in the corner behind Ms De'ath's desk for all of the paperwork and equipment she did not want left in danger in a drawer.

The classroom tingled with anticipation as they all waited for the signal, feigning concentration on the lecture they were receiving about poetic techniques. The sun burned brighter than ever through the windows, and for the first time Foz noticed there were streaks of white slashing through her black mane of hair.

The second observation he made was almost enough to make him stop what was about to take place; the flask was missing.

Why had she not brought the flask? Or at least, why was it not on her desk? Was she conceding defeat?

But then she turned her back for a moment and, with one sweeping motion involving tip-toes to reach the highest writing, wiped the blackboard clean of similes.

Foz coughed.

Kev felt time slow down as Ms De'ath turned back to face the room, noticing the dust of ancient chalk settling in the air as the light intercepted its fall from the board rubber. She began to speak again, scanning the room for the one kid who looked panicked that they hadn't written everything down.

From his seat at the back, Fat Knacker felt a sense of achievement and imagined this were similar to how it looked when Freddie had gazed out at thousands of people clapping along to Radio Gaga in unison.

Dave tried his best to stay in time and avoid getting over-excited.

Ms De'ath stopped scanning and stood very still. From her position, looking forward, it felt as though she were at sea. The whole class, from that vile young man at the front of her desk, to those swots at the back, were swaying, in time, ever-so slightly. Each student was perhaps moving no more than two inches in total; just enough to be noticeable. All of their faces were studious and enquiring, pens in hand as though oblivious to their own movement.

She hated kids. Not just horrible gangs of thugs like some of these, but all of them. She had no way of knowing exactly who had started this, or why, or if it was really happening, or if it was her who was swaying, or if the school was moving, or if she kept making tea instead of coffee, or anything.

She left. Right there and then, Ms De'ath picked up her bag, turned to her right, walked across the room, out of the door and was gone. They all sat perfectly still, scared to even look around.

After ten, maybe fifteen minutes, another teacher came in to investigate the sheer volume in the notoriously quiet classroom. He then sent someone to the office, and a few minutes later another teacher came in and whispered something to him. He looked at her and said, without the thought to whisper back, 'gone?'

And that was the last they saw of her. According to a kid in year nine whose Ma taught at the school, she had literally walked out of the classroom, straight to her car, and gone. The school could not contact her, and she did not contact them. The school, therefore, did not know what had happened.

'Do you think we went too far?', asked Dave that weekend, sitting on the hill by the VG. They were taking it in turns to pass around Hughesy's new Discman, that was entirely portable but only played CDs without jumping if you kept it completely motionless. Kev had declined in favour of his trusty Walkman, so wasn't listening to the conversation at all.

'Maybe.'

'What? No. We did nothing bad - we just made her feel bad, like she did. We made her feel less; if she went mental then good. If she realised she's hated then good - maybe she'll be nicer to people now!'

'What would you do if you saw her?'

'I wouldn't recognise her, me! Never taught me - just know she's got that wild black hair like an electrocuted cat!'

'Serious, Cookie? You never had the displeasure?'

'Na - I'm just lucky, I guess. She grassed me to the Head once for messing about with water bombs, but I didn't meet with her.'

'Is that when you were throwing them at Knacky?'

'Yeah - couldn't miss!'

'Dickhead! I looked like I'd pissed myself.'

'You would piss yourself if the walk to the loo was too far, you spanner!'

'Nice to have you put in an appearance, by the way!'

'It's a celebration, isn't it!'

'Rights is it!'

'Look at all this, lads - the world is our playground again and we will always be free to do what we want and go where we want to go!'

'Let's get drinking then!'

'Bucky and Mitch have gone to the shop to ask someone to go in!'

'As if we're trusting stoned Zig and Zag...'

Standing there in the dark, amidst the shattered glass, Cookie held on tightly to Knacker's shoulder, thankful for his solidity. Behind them, they heard shouting and the crashing of bodies against wood. In front, the huge man glared at them, a trickle of blood running from the centre of his mouth, and took a step forward.

Fat Knacker stepped forward too, putting his mask back on, his sheer size forcing itself out of the horrid lycra at every opportunity, staring at the figure towering above him.

No words were spoken, but it was clear from Cookie's vantage point that the man understood Knacker wasn't going to let him get to his friend. His stature seemed bigger, more confident, almost intimidating. Instead, the hulk turned and knelt down next to the old lady.

Appearing in the glassless frame above and behind them, Lee suddenly exclaimed, 'Knacker, what the fuck are you doing here?'

The unusual figure on the ground turned slightly toward Lee as he swore, and Bucky flinched at the sight of the bloody trail falling from its scarred face onto the white hair of the woman who had spoken to him at the door moments earlier.

Lights filled the garden next door, as a man, holding his wife and son back as though from a fire, peered through his destroyed fence at them. 'Do you need the police?' he asked, to none of them in particular.

The beast on the floor answered simply 'no', to their surprise.

'Is Death dead?', asked Gaz, straining to look past Lee and Bucky.

'Think so', said Lee.

'No.'

'He's a man of many words, isn't he!' uttered Kev, as Mitch silenced him.

'Can we erm…come through your house mate?', Knacker asked the neighbour, gesturing to Cookie and himself. 'There's no back door!'

'Wait...is that it?'

'Is what what?'

'Everyone just walks away and it's all over?', questioned Gaz.

'Dude, this isn't a horror story!'

As they shuffled towards the light, over the fence, Knacker looked back at the man as he passed Ms De'ath, lying over both of his arms, face up, through the window frame and stepped back in.

Back out the front of the houses, on the private, gated road, Cookie told them some of what had happened.

'You didn't recognise her?'

'I didn't know the woman!'

'We pranked the shit out of that fucking bitch!', replied Kev.

'Don't need to swear so much, mate!'

'Alright, Da!'

'Sorry, I guess I don't feel like being profane. Lads, I'm sorry I went off on one earlier. I love you guys!'

'Shirtlifter!'

'Shut up, Dave!'

'Naw, in all seriousness, ditto lads!'

'Come on, let's get away from here in case they do actually call the police!'

'Where to?'

'Only one place to end the night - VG!'

'Actually, yeah - I've got something we need to do as well...before the VG!'

'What's that then, Hughesy?'

'You'll see! Follow me.''

Chapter 30: Ashes

All together, except Lee who was sat on the floor a few metres away, by unanimous vote, the men looked out over the town.

'Lads, there's a six pack of fucking Ace here!'

'That's ours...'

'Forgot about that. Guess we got distracted discussing the failings of modern society, eh?'

'I forgot you'd all been up here already.'

'It's a hell of a view.'

'Foz loved it up here, lads, and that's why I think it's a good place for doing this...' Hughesy pulled from his jacket the metal can given to him by Foz's Ma. 'She...well, 'they' she said...didn't know where to scatter these!'

'Shit, is that Foz?'

'I thought you were gonna pull out a camping stove and make us some beans, mate.'

'Has he been with us since before Kev became a crash test dummy?'

'He has.'

'Why didn't you say?'

'I just didn't know what to say. Lads, I've got our dead marra in me pocket?'

'Fair enough. Do you not think the VG would be better?'

'And have little mingers and chavs fucking around on him?'

'He'd at least be with millions of dead little Cookie's!'

'Rank!'

'I was thinking, seeing as you made that big speech in the pub, you'd say a few words, Lee?'

'Dress like a paedo and suddenly you're giving a sermon!'

'I guess I can...'

'I promise not to touch your shoulder!'

'Right, grab a drink!'

As the lads opened the cans of Ace, Lee stared out at the town beneath them. It was much darker now, and much darker than it had ever looked in their youth, but so was life.

Kev, Cookie and Mitch refused an offer of a can, so the others had one each.

Lee began. 'Life should be nearing its middle for us, not already being over. I've not got my head around losing Foz, and I don't think I ever will. Thing is, I don't think we should. It should remain unresolved inside us to remind us of the pain and happiness that person represents, don't you think? I don't want to get used to the idea because I don't want to stop thinking about him. If nothing else, he's brought us together again in a way he always did. The one we relied on, who we rang and waited for, who we all can't think of a memory without him in it. More than a friend, he's now our teenage years, dead and gone and still so awesome. Without him, life then would have been so different, and with him now it would be different again. He was a closed door that didn't open in time. I love him, and I love all of you so much; we need to remember this moment, and I think we will *all* remember this night, and make sure we stay together this time. For now, and forever, to Foz!'

'To Foz!'

'Foz lad!'

'Foz...'

'The wanker!'

Chapter 31: Eight Doors

In the dark of night, the ridiculous neon orange sign looked more ridiculous, and the maniacally smiling cartoon face staring helplessly out of the 'O' in Happy Shopper was even more maniacal.

On the hill closest to the narrow pool of water to the left of the shop, just before you reached the little metal bridge, a number of figures cast silhouettes against the night sky.

Lying half on his side, with one leg bent up and one elbow propping his body from the grass itself, Cookie was more relieved than he had ever known possible. He took his dented hip flask from his right pocket (realising he did still have his phone), and had a swig. It was 23:53.

'I'm done drinking after this, you know - turn over a new one. I'm not even angry at Lee.'

'Me? Why would you be?'

'You called me a fucking roidhead gay, didn't you!'

Dave laughed.

'Gaz?', asked Hughesy. 'What song did Foz disappear behind the curtain to? His Ma couldn't remember.'

'That's a shock!'

'It was Oasis' *Live Forever.*'

'He will.'

'He will for her, anyway!'

'Dickhead!'

The group all smiled.

'I can't believe all of that has happened to everyone tonight, just from playing Nicky Nocky Nine Doors!'

'The Invitational Knock Cup, wasn't it, Bucky?'

'Foz Tribute Nicky Nocky Nine Doors Open Tournament, if you must know!'

'What are you lot on about?'

'What?'

'Who's been playing Knocky Doorsy?'

'Fuck right off with that - that's nearly as bad as Knock Upon Thy Neighbour or whatever it was!'

'Gaz, are you for real?'

'What? Yeah!'

'We all have!'
'Is that why we've been to all them houses?'
'Yeah!'
'Gaz the Spaz never lets us down, does he!'
'Can't say that nowadays!'
'Sorry…'
'Retard will suffice!'
'We've all had our turn, Gaz.'
'I don't want to miss out!'
'Well, it's a bit late now.'
Checking his backlit Casio watch, he replied excitedly, 'I'll be back!'

Gaz ran around the narrow pond to the VG and vanished, reappearing seconds later. From their position they couldn't see the shop door, but they heard an inaudible shout followed by the metal slamming against its frame.

'Done!', wheezed Gaz. 'And I found this…' holding up a bag of shopping.

Gaz, I think you are the only person who has successfully knocked, annoyed the occupant, and ran away clean.'

'Lee certainly didn't!'

Lee, sat about ten feet from the others, gave them two fingers and smiled.

'Don't know about you lot, but I need to get home to bed - I'm fucked!', said Cookie.

'It's been a bit of a bust, hasn't it!'

'Are you kidding? Foz would have loved this - all these mad stories to tell people - it's been right up his street tonight!'

'True!'

'And although it hasn't gone entirely to plan…'

'Understatement!'

'…we're here together.'

'I hope it is a long, long time before we do something like this again, chaps. No offence, but I'm happy seeing you're all well on Facebook!'

'Haha I agree.'

'Unless we can arrange a nice poker night, or a meal or something?'

'We're not dating, bender!', responded Dave.

'Why don't we just stay here tonight? It's dry, it's warm, we're already here!'

'You think we should all just stay together?'

'Fuck yeah - lads forever, man!

'I've got kids!'

'You've not said, pal, really?'

'Yeah, and it's work tomorrow for me!'

'Okay, group chat tomorrow, but for now, goodnight!'

'I'll walk with you.'

'Me too - later, lads.'

As Cookie, Hughesy and Gaz walked over the hill and out of sight, heading towards the small wooden bridge, Kev got to his feet.

'You want me to take the wheelbarrow? And Knacker, do you want a lift?'

'I'll take the 'barrow, lads - I just live over there.'

'Cheers, Dave.'

'Are you okay to drive; you drank a canny bit!'

'Aye, and then I went full Evel Knievel on some poor fuck's door and sobered up pretty quickly!'

'Yeah, go on then.'

'Do you know you've not been for a piss or shit since?'

'Really? Oh yeah...'

'Will you drop me off, I don't want to be seen walking around covered in shit!'

'Are you fuck getting in my car like that!'

'It's your shit!'

'Don't care - piss off!'

Fat Knacker, picking the last cold chicken from the bones and dropping them into the carrier bag, said his goodbyes and walked with Kev over to the car park behind the VG. As the engine revved '...are the children of the...' blasted briefly before Kev turned it off. Waving as they pulled away, the headlights illuminating the remaining four for a second, they were gone.

'Right, you need anything out of here? If not, I'm away lads.'

'No, cheers Dave - I'll get that back off you at some point. Night mate.'

'I'm going to head back to Marie's!'

'You'll wake the kids, dude!'

'No, I've been texting her - she's watching out for me! That's why I'm not drinking anymore, you know, so I last. See you soon, eh?'

'Hope not!'

'Bye mate.'

'Dave, hold up!'

As Mitch jogged after Dave, and the squeaking of the wheel gradually faded, Bucky and Lee lay back on the hill.

'Kev said 'nothing untoward will happen'. You hear him say that? Right at the start of the night?'

'I don't know - he was wrong.'

'Too right. Some scary shit!'

'Some funny shit!'

'Some actual shit!'

'That too.'

'Can you believe choices as teenagers come back to bite you on the arse twenty-odd years on?'

'But it's the choices for mates that have seen us through tonight.'

'Wish Foz had been here...like, in human form rather than as tinned goods...'

They both stared across the narrow pond at the VG for a while; perhaps they could see the shadows of ten friends laughing and carrying on, or perhaps they were lost in their own separate memories of Foz, or their own thoughts for the future.

'It's an immense, profound sadness, isn't it?'

'Knowing he's gone?'

'Yeah. I can't quite get my head around it.'

'Whether you've spent time together or not over the years, I don't think you ever lose the love you had for your childhood best mates, you know!'

'I agree - and there's a huge part of me that's just wishing I had spoken to him, or he had text me, or we'd bumped into each other one more time.'

'You feel like that could have been the difference, don't you. One slightly different event and other things may not have unfolded the way they did - like you personally could have, and should have, been able to prevent it.'

'Couldn't put it better, mate.'

'It's overwhelming...grief comes in waves and you try not to feel it, then it's a tsunami when you finally open that door - it manifests into a monster and then you're acting like a twat!'

'You think everyone's okay?'

'I doubt they'll want to meet up for a while, but yeah. They'd say if they weren't, right?'

'You would hope.'

'I guess we have to make more of an effort to stay in touch…'

'By texts or chats; not via Facebook. That's a veil for real life isn't it!'

'I guess it can be.'

'You know what Foz's last post was?'

'What?'

'He shared a video of 'We Built This City…'

'Decent.'

'…on sausage rolls!'

'Haha fuck, man! Imagine that being your final post - we don't have famous last words any more do we…'

'No, and we don't have conversations with the people we should - those lads, even you covered in shit! You all mean so much to me.'

'Same mate. We making a move?'

'Time to go, yeah.'

As they stood, Lee put his arm around Bucky's shoulders, who pushed him away instantly. Lee came back, both of them laughing, and put his arm around his shoulders again, this time with Bucky reciprocating. The two of them, one of them in a colour-changing t-shirt and the other in shitty paedo-pants, crossed the little metal bridge, walked around the boating lake's right hand edge, and into the path next to the primary school fence where Foz had always appeared. In the dark, surrounded by houses and canopied by trees, they faded from view.

Chapter 33: Nine Doors.

As he trundled the wheelbarrow, with remnants of cider and alcopops lingering around it, toward the big bridge, Mitch caught up with him.

'Where are you going?' asked Dave.

'Mate...no grief...I'm heading to Marie's!'

'Oh you'll wake the bairns!'

'She's watching out for me - we've been messaging.'

'Good for you - nice to see you not being gay as fuck for your car!'

'Car's a girl, for a start! And you are one massive homophobe, do you know that?'

'Woah - how come?'

'You just throw gay and faggot insults out all the time - for someone in a Spice Girls t-shirt, it's a bit ironic!'

'Ah, bollocks - I've forgotten to get my top out of Kev's car...I'm not homophobic.'

'I know mate, I'm kidding.'

'Good. Bender!'

'Haha, will your missus be up still?'

'Erm...no I would think not now; it is nearly midnight!'

'Yeah, fair point.'

'I'm going this way.'

'It's been good to see you, dude!'

'Same - a pint sometime soon?'

'Yeah - you live up there?'

'Aye.'

'Played it risky tonight haven't you - harassing people in your own estate!'

'I'm sure I'll be alright.'

'Hope you weren't seen.'

'No chance. Say 'hi' to Marie.'

'Will do...later mate...'

Dave and Mitch hugged, which they'd never done, and Mitch turned and walked along the side of the beck towards the little wooden bridge, before turning left and disappearing between two houses. Looking back along the long, too-straight path toward the VG, Dave thought he saw the shadows of Bucky and Lee, arms around each other's shoulders, framed against the orange neon glow of the Happy Shopper sign. Then, they were gone.

Dave smiled to himself, and squeaked his way along the alleyway that faced the bridge. He turned into the street with the vomit-stained wheelie bin, then turned into a cul-de-sac. He picked up the wheelbarrow as he passed his own gate, trying not to awaken his partner.

Placing it carefully down on the grass to the right of his front door, he pulled his key from his flares and silently slid it into the lock. Stepping in and closing it noiselessly behind him, he glanced up the stairs on his right and took a step towards them.

'I'm in here!'

'What are you doing up?'

'I wanted to make sure you got in safe!'

'What? Why?'

'Been a bunch of little bastards knocking on the door all night!'

'Really?'

'Yeah. Four times. It stopped around nine-thirty but I was worried about you.'

'No need...I've been fine. Home now, eh?'

'Yeah, sorry, don't know why I was worrying.'

'Sure we won't get any more trouble from young'uns as well.'

'Okay, okay...how was the send-off? It looks like you've taught your face to smile again.'

'Yeah...I was telling someone earlier I thought I wouldn't laugh ever again.'

'Glad you have...was it good?'

'Really good...different...but good.'

'He deserved that. He was a good man. We'll have to check on his Mam.'

'Yeah, actually Hughesy popped in to see her.'

'That's good. She the same?'

'Seemed to be from what he said.'

'Poor woman.'

'May be a blessing you know, not knowing Foz and Morris are both gone!'

'That's idiotic!'

'Hmm, I guess.'

'So, did you tell them?'

'Well, no I didn't, actually…'

'They should just accept you for who you are, David! Foz did!'

'They would - it's not that I don't want to, or can't...I nearly did a few times... suppose it's about altering the past, and everything they remember about me...that sound stupid?'

'No, it doesn't. Come here. I just hope you weren't still doing that over-the-top offensive diversion tactic you utilised when we first met!'

'I may have regressed slightly.'

'It makes me sad, that in losing Foz you also lost your only link between who you are and who you were.'

'That's a bit deep for this time of night.'

'Right, you coming straight up to bed then?'

'Yeah.'

Dave and his husband left the living room, and began to walk upstairs. 'Tell me everything tomorrow?'

'Maybe.'

'Except one thing I need to know right now - where's that hideous tank top gone?'

'Oh, it's in Kev's car. It got stained.'

'Did you even ask if you could take that t-shirt?'

'This isn't a Take That t-shirt!'

Chapter 33: An End

Had you the ability to look down from above the town around midnight on that Saturday night, you would have seen a glowing orange square and an expanse of glittering moonlit water. From the left of this nine figures had emanated and dispersed.

Two of these figures had moved to the right and entered a vehicle above the orange square, which had then reversed out and driven up through a winding road in an ex- council estate. At the end of this road, the vehicle had turned left and driven along the perimeter of a mass of fields and a park.

Another two figures had left to the top right, arm in arm, and disappeared beneath a tunnel of trees.

A reddish figure bigger than the others had left with two others to the top left, skirting the shimmering water and crossing a small dark bridge. The three had separated and disappeared into the maze of alleys and streets.

One with a wheelbarrow had left along a long, straight path, chased down by another. They had stood still next to a larger bridge for a moment, before coming together and then going separate ways.

You would be forgiven for thinking, for the briefest of seconds, that a tenth figure had remained on the grass to the left of the orange glowing square.

If you had this ability, you would have lingered long enough to see a group of six figures and one smaller, possibly female, figure step out in front of one of the separated friends.

You would have seen a coming together, followed by all but one figure sprinting from the area.

You would have seen this lone figure slump, its legs splaying out in front of it on the ground in a v-shape.

If you had the ability to swoop down, you would have heard their last gasping words. 'We should have stayed together...lads forever...'

an end

What happened to Foz may not be explicit - it doesn't need to be. Your friends and family love you.

If you're feeling like you want to die, it's important to tell someone. Help and support is available right now if you need it. You do not have to struggle with difficult feelings alone.

Phone a helpline

These free helplines are there to help when you're feeling down or desperate.

Samaritans - for everyone

Call 116 123

Campaign Against Living Miserably (CALM)

Call 0800 58 58 58 – 5pm to midnight every day

Papyrus – for people under 35

Call 0800 068 41 41 – 9am to midnight every day

Childline – for children and young people under 19

Call 0800 1111 – the number will not show up on your phone bill

SOS Suicide of Silence – for everyone

Call 0300 1020 505 – 9am to midnight every day

Message a text line

If you do not want to talk to someone over the phone, these text lines are open 24 hours a day, every day.

Shout Crisis Text Line – for everyone

Text "SHOUT" to 85258

YoungMinds Crisis Messenger – for people under 19

Text "YM" to 85258

Talk to someone you trust

Let family or friends know what's going on for you. They may be able to offer support and help keep you safe.

There's no right or wrong way to talk about suicidal feelings – starting the conversation is what's important.

Who else you can talk to

If you find it difficult to talk to someone you know, you could:

- call a GP – ask for an emergency appointment
- call 111 out of hours – they will help you find the support and help you need
- contact your mental health crisis team – dependent on your local area

Printed in Great Britain
by Amazon